Million Dollar Staircase

ISBN-13: 978-0692603307

ISBN-10: 0692603301

Front Cover Photography by David Crosby/Crosby Stills

Cover art by SwoonWorthy Book Covers

Printed in the United States of America

Million Dollar Staircase

A Will Harper Novel

David Crosby

Published by

CROSBY Stills

Thanks to the Plantation Writers Guild for their input and especially for their encouragement in the writing of this book, and to all my beta readers for their help with catching errors. Any that remain are my own.

This book is dedicated to my wonderful wife Marilyn,

who has always believed in me.

Chapter One

It was a beautiful day at the Dolphin River Marina, and Sandy St. Martin danced in the sunshine.

"Will, this is amazing news! I didn't know how much longer I could hold on with the way business has been, but this changes everything."

I'd come over by water in my little Boston Whaler runabout to bring her a copy of the Bradenton Herald, the closest thing to a local paper in the small town of Dolphin River, Florida. I had to admit, the news on the headline of the business section was indeed amazing.

It read "Dolphin River to get $65 Million Development along Riverfront," and the attached map showed it surrounding the area where Sandy's marina was located. She was beyond exuberant.

"A hotel, restaurants, shops and a *reever* walk, all located on either side of my marina. *Merde!* I'm going to get rich!" Her French accent always got heavier when she was excited.

"Whoa, slow down girl. It seems odd to me that this project could get put together all around your land without you even knowing about it. Before you start counting the money, I'd call the developer and see how their plans affect you." She looked crestfallen, and I said, "Hey, I'm not trying to rain on your parade, but developers usually have the money split up among themselves and their investors before they even break ground. You need to make sure you aren't getting screwed in this deal."

She sighed, put a hand on my shoulder and said, "*Oui*, I know you're right. This just seemed like a miracle though. Can't I celebrate a little?"

I gave her a hug. "Sure you can. It's got to be an improvement, right?"

Hopefully it would be, but my experience writing about local politics left me doubtful. I'd been a journalist before leaving the crumbling world of newspapers in disgust, and it seemed that the little guys always got screwed in development projects. It was the money people who made out like bandits, and they didn't much care about collateral damage.

Sandy was a sweetheart, and I hated to see her get taken advantage of. She was one of the first people I met when I quit my newspaper job, moved to Florida, and bought a boat to live on. I'd been looking for a liveaboard space when I discovered her little marina, which unfortunately didn't have a big enough slip open for my Grand Banks trawler. I'd ended up at the more upscale Sailfin Point Marina in nearby Palmetto, Florida, just off the Manatee River.

She let me stay at the fuel dock for a couple of days while I found another berth for my boat, the WanderLust, and we'd gotten to be good friends since then. Sandy and I got together every week or so for dinner and drinks, either on my trawler or on her sailboat, a beautiful Beneteau First 40 model named Au Revoir. We weren't in a romance, just a friendship, but there was a definite attraction between the two of us.

Both of us were nervous about getting more involved. I'd only been divorced for a few years after a lousy marriage, and she had quit a long term relationship when she came to Florida from St. Martin, the island her French parents had moved her to when she was in her teens. Getting serious with anyone seemed like a dangerous path to us both. For now we were happy to have a friend of the opposite sex to spend time with, while avoiding the mine field of a romance.

In the meantime, I hated watching her struggle to keep her business going. Marinas like hers have a difficult regulatory environment to operate in, with the EPA watching like a hawk for fuel spills. The city building codes people were constantly after her to make electrical and plumbing upgrades to her somewhat dated facilities, and the bank was after her to catch up on her mortgage payments. Sandy operated on a razor thin margin, and when something needed repairing, the money wasn't always there. This new riverfront development could make the difference for her, finally providing the money she needed to improve the place and to bring in a better class of customers.

I was still uneasy that she'd been left out of the planning

by the developers, and felt like it didn't bode well. We made plans for her to come to my boat for dinner that evening, and she waved goodbye as I pulled my little Whaler away from the dock. I puttered into the river channel and glanced at the rusty gear on the gas dock and the peeling paint on the marina's concrete block office. It didn't look like something that would go with the sketches of the $65 million dollar river front complex we'd seen in the paper. The architectural drawing left a blank area that included where Sandy's marina was located, with TBD stamped on it. The question was, to be determined by whom?

§

As I left the Dolphin River and made my way up the larger Manatee River towards Sailfin Point, I looked at the beautiful waters between Palmetto and Bradenton. I couldn't help but marvel at how different my life was from just a year earlier. In 2014 I'd been slogging my way through my job at a Georgia newspaper, living in a small apartment, scraping by financially as I worked to pay my bills and pay alimony to my ex wife. Now I lived on a beautiful boat, which was both my home and my office.

I'd abandoned the newspaper business before it dried up completely, and now spent my days working on the novel that had percolated in the back of my mind for the last decade. It really is true that if you want to hear God laugh, tell him your plans. I'd always believed that change was good, even bad change, because it eventually led to something better. My divorce was a good example. I had been a faithful sort and believed in the whole "Till Death do Us Part" shtick, so splitting up wasn't on

4

my agenda. My wife had other plans and I wasn't part of them.

Laughing at the irony of it, I reflected on the fact that I'd been nearly broke when we divorced, thus her small alimony. That had changed drastically the following year, but it had been too late for my ex, Julie, to share in the windfall. Karma's a bitch, you know?

As I neared the marina and my home at slip F-11, my reverie was interrupted by Captain Rick passing me in his skiff.

"Hey Rick, where you headed?" I shouted across the water between our boats.

He pulled up beside me and said, "Just going across the bay to check a few of my traps. I thought crabs for dinner sounded good."

Tampa Bay didn't have the best crabs, but if you could catch them, the price was right.

"When you get back, stop by the boat and have a beer with me." I knew he couldn't resist free beer and I wanted to pick his brain about the city's plans for Dolphin River. Rick was a retired ship's captain who lived on my dock and seemed to know everything that went on in this community, and I thought having more information might be a help to Sandy.

"I should be back in two or three hours, Will, I'll stop by for sure."

We waved our goodbyes, and I continued into the marina off the Manatee, past the breakwater to where the rows of slips held boats like a crowded parking lot. When I got nearer to my slip, I idled slowly towards it, partly to avoid rocking the other boats, and partly because I never tired of admiring the beautiful boat I called home.

What a difference a year makes.

Chapter Two

My path to a life on the water had been a roundabout one. I did the usual things; high school girlfriends, went off to college, married a girl just before graduation, and thought my life was all set. I got a degree in Journalism from the University of Georgia and set off to conquer the world as an investigative reporter, new wife in tow. It didn't take me long to find out that school was a lot different than the real world.

Newspapers are supported by advertising and no publisher wants to alienate the people who pay the bills. So stories get killed, great ideas get shot down, and the search for truth that I learned about in college didn't exist anymore. Technology and the internet had eroded the news business nationwide over the past few years, with constant layoffs and salary cuts. By the third year I was already burned out but stayed on to support my wife's ever growing shopping habit.

Julie was insecure, to be honest, about pretty much everything. She hadn't finished college, she struggled with her weight, and at a height of four feet and eleven inches she looked up at most people. Life just didn't seem to be much fun for her. I did my best to help her find happiness, but she seemed to prefer her American Express Gold card to the sentimental cards and flowers I brought home to her. I loved her, but was beginning to see that it was one sided. When we were still in school I found out she'd slept with my college roommate when I was out of town, but I'd forgiven her and thought it was a one-time thing.

Imagine my surprise when I came home early from a road trip for the paper and found her in bed with her boss. Julie worked at an insurance company, but stupid me, I'd believed the "working late" stories she told. I guess that explained why she was never in the mood for sex with me. My naiveté went away when the marriage did. The divorce was painful, in part, because all she wanted was money. I thought she cared at least a little, but it turns out I was just a walking credit card. I don't mean to sound bitter, it was a learning experience after all. In spite of her infidelity, fighting a divorce is a long, expensive process, and I ended up settling for a small monthly alimony payment rather than years of court battles.

The newspaper job had become almost as empty as the marriage was, but I got myself transferred to the lifestyle section so I could at least quit pretending we were searching for truth. Writing feature stories about local characters was a little more fun, but I was counting the years until the alimony ended and I could take to the road. I was not going to settle for being disappointed with my life.

God does watch out for us even when we're not paying attention, and I sure wasn't listening for His Divine Intervention when the doorbell rang.

It was a FedEx envelope from an attorney in Macon, Georgia, with a letter telling me that he regretted to inform me of the death of my great aunt Dorothy. I remembered Dotty well, my Mom's cousin who always seemed like a close part of our family. I'd been dutiful in my visits to her over the years, although getting by there once a year was my idea of dutiful. I lived several hours from her, and it just wasn't a trip we made very often. She was sad when I got divorced, and I'd only seen her twice since then. Now she was gone and I'd have no more chances for a visit.

OK, at this point you're probably saying "What is this story about? This guy's life sucks!"

And if it ended here, you'd be right. What had started with great promise was not turning out well. Dotty's will changed all of that.

"Dear Mr. Harper, we regret to inform you of the death of your relative Dorothy Townsend. She designated you as the recipient of the bulk of her estate, including her home, her car (A 1992 Buick) and the title to her land holdings in Wilkinson County, Georgia. They consist of two tracts of approximately 200 acres each. One of the tracts is currently being mined for bauxite under lease to MineCo Corporation of Georgia. Please call for further details. Sincerely, John G. Whelchell, Attorney at Law."

Wow. I knew from talking to my parents that Dotty had

died, but I certainly never expected an inheritance. It was still office hours, and since I had an early interview scheduled for the next morning, I'd taken the afternoon off. I picked up the phone and dialed Mr. Whelchell, reaching his secretary. She put me right through to him.

"Yes, Mr. Whelchell, this is Will Harper. I just got your Fedex. I'm pretty shocked that she left her estate to me."

"It's not usually a surprise to heirs when they are mentioned in the will, but without a spouse or children she named you in hers. I helped her with the changes to her will in her final days, and she seemed quite fond of you. She said she could count on you to use the money to live out your dreams."

I had to sit down at that. "I'm speechless." I took a minute to gather my composure. "I don't know what I ever did to make her have that much faith in me, but I'll try to honor her wishes."

I paused for a minute to gather myself, and the lawyer filled the silence. "Miss Townsend told me you dreamed of travel, so I don't imagine you'd want to live in the house. It's in a very old section of town, so it's valuable, and our firm can handle the sale of the home and the contents if you like."

Living in a one bedroom apartment in Atlanta sure didn't allow me space for a house full of antiques, so that sounded like the best plan to me. I hated to ask, but it seemed like an obvious question.

"Do you have an estimated value of the house and the furnishings?"

"The market isn't the best right now, but that is a very desirable area. I'd say $300,000 for the house and another

$50,000 for the furniture. She was quite an antique collector."

I was sitting on the arm of my couch, and his statement startled me so much I lost my balance and fell to the floor. "Are you saying it's worth $350,000?"

"Well, there will be real estate fees and auction costs, but you should net around $325,000. Then there's the income from the mining."

"Income?" I was starting to wonder if I was imagining this phone call.

"Yes, they dig pits for the bauxite, and when it's removed it's weighed as they truck it to the plant. It's used in fracking for oil, very hot right now, you know. You'll be paid based on the weight. I believe it's currently running between three and four dollars a ton."

Three or four dollars a ton? I thought that was in the category of fill dirt. My dreams of riches seemed to be going up in smoke. "Can you give me a bottom line on that?"

"Well, it fluctuates with the digging weather, the demand at the plant, and how big the deposit is that they are working. Last year Miss Townsend received $220,000 in royalties."

I sat back down again with a thud. Whelchell took my silence as a need for more information.

"Of course, you can't ever be sure of the totals. It's been as little as $160,000 and as much as $285,000 over the last ten years."

I finally croaked out a question. "How long is this expected to last?"

"They've only mined about a third of the 200 acres so far.

If the deposit holds out I'd say another 15 to 20 years."

Holy crap. It was time to quit my job and buy a boat.

Chapter Three

Things never happen as fast as you hope they will, but you can at least get off to a quick start. I went into the newsroom the next morning and told my editor that I was leaving for a life of travel. He could barely be bothered to lift his eyes from the wire stories he was scanning and didn't much care what my reason was.

"No problem, we're about to cut staff for the third time this year. Don't bother working a notice."

I hadn't expected that he'd ask me to stay, but was still startled at how fast the newspaper industry was collapsing around us. Most dailies were becoming ghost towns, with a skeleton crew to report local news while the wire services provided everything else. I was getting out just in time, while there was still a job to walk away from.

I packed up my desk, said goodbye to the few friends still with reporting jobs, and headed for my car. I felt a little sad at not just leaving my career behind, but at the demise of a once great industry.

Boats had been my first love, which was surprising since I grew up in Atlanta, a long way from the water unless you counted man-made lakes. My only knowledge of real boating came from visits to Florida when I was a child, visiting my grandparents in Fort Lauderdale. I was intrigued by the drawbridges, traffic backing up as the steel grids rose in the air like skyscrapers, moving the roadbed out of the way for ships, tugboats, sailboats and cabin cruisers. I often wondered where they were going, and envied them the journey.

I'd been an avid reader growing up, in love with the language of words. I guess that came naturally to me. My father had taken me to the library every Saturday, and I was allowed to check out two books, which usually only lasted me a couple of days. Everyone in my family spent a lot of time immersed in books, so it was part of our daily routine. Being a lifelong reader gave me the freedom to travel the world in my imagination, going places and doing things that are only possible on the printed page. Some physical things are out of reach for most folks, like taking a trip to the moon, but you can read about those who have made the journey. Within the confines of gravity, however, I was determined to go places and explore, and a boat seemed like a great way to do it.

Now, unexpectedly, I had the means to make that dream a reality.

The next step would be finding a boat. That was something that would be impossible in landlocked Atlanta, so I booked a flight to Fort Lauderdale. South Florida is full of marinas and boat dealers, so I'd have plenty to choose from. I hadn't received the bulk of my inheritance yet, as Dotty's house was still for sale, but there had been enough cash in her bequest to fund my search and make a down payment on a boat.

I thought with a chuckle about all of the money Dotty had been earning off the mining proceeds for the past ten years. When I asked the attorney, somewhat indelicately, what had become of it, he'd chuckled and said, "She turned the idea of tithing on its head. She kept ten per cent for living expenses, and donated the rest to the Episcopal Church she attended." Giving it away had made her happy, and that was a good thing.

In the meantime, I'd been doing research online for the best boat for me, and I was thinking of a trawler style yacht. Now you might think my new found wealth would mean I could buy a real yacht, as in multiple decks and helicopter landing pads, but I wouldn't have that kind of money. Heck, I couldn't even buy a new trawler, as they are easily over a half million dollars. My plan was to buy a 15 to 20 year old boat, put it in like-new shape, and spend my days on the water. The income provided by the estate would fund my travels, but I thought it would be a mistake to blow all the cash on the boat itself, since fuel, dockage and maintenance can add up in a hurry. I'd searched the internet for likely prospects, and already had a list of boats to look at.

My flight was an early one at Atlanta's Hartsfield airport, and the air was chilly as I made my way from the parking deck to the check-in desk. I had a light wind breaker over my Hawaiian style shirt and my cargo shorts, but my feet were freezing in mesh sandals. I was traveling light, just a duffle with a change of clothes and toiletries, and didn't have room for a set of warmer clothes. The South Florida forecast was 80 degrees and sunny so the chill wouldn't last long. I was ushered to the front of the line, a perk I wasn't used to. Flying first class was a treat I was giving myself for the start of this adventure, and I was hoping it would be worth it.

When I boarded the plane first in line and was ushered into a cushy leather seat I started to feel like it had been a good investment. As the peasants in the back rows filed past me, struggling with their massive carry-ons, I almost felt guilty. That is, until the flight attendant stopped at my seat.

"Can I get you a drink sir?"

"You mean before we take off ?"

"Yes sir, that's something we do for our first class passengers." She included a dazzling smile in her spiel.

"Sure, why not. Could I get a Bloody Mary?"

"I'll have it for you right away sir."

OK, now I was hooked. The rest of the flight was just as pleasant. I'd had to fly fairly often for assignments in my newspaper work, but *never* first class. If they'd had a steerage section that's where management would have put us. Newspapers don't believe in spending money on lowly reporters, and the photographers have it even worse. Susie, my flight attendant, was at my beck and call during the trip, right down to the hot towel she brought for me to wipe my hands and face with after my drinks and snack. I could get used to this.

We touched down in Fort Lauderdale less than two hours

after takeoff, and the view over the waves as we made our approach was amazing. The sun sparkled off the waters of the Atlantic, and I could see canals lined with boats weaving through the neighborhoods near the ocean. I was ready for this adventure to begin.

With no checked bags I was in my rental car quickly and headed for the boat broker's office. He would be showing me five of his listings that day, and I was eager to get started.

By the time we'd seen the fourth boat I was getting discouraged. The limits of my price range meant the boats were smaller than I preferred or not well kept. The last one on the list was older than my preference, but at least it should be big enough. It was a 1996 Marine Trader, a 47 foot motor yacht. It looked good sitting at the dock behind a canal side home, and when I stepped aboard I thought this might be the one.

The main salon had teak parquet floors, a couch and two overstuffed chairs, and a galley a couple of steps down with a nearly full-size refrigerator and stove. The master cabin had a queen-size bed, something almost unheard of on a boat, and three of the walls were lined with mirrors to give a feeling of openness. With built-in dressers and a closet it was the biggest cabin I'd seen on a boat yet. The private bath was small but workable. In the bow was a vee shaped berth with a double bed and a small bathroom, called a head in nautical terms.

The rear deck was completely enclosed by windowed canvas and had a varnished teak deck. A couple of steps up from there was the flybridge, with a cushy chair for the captain to sit in while piloting the boat. In spite of being almost 20 years old, the boat was immaculate. Even better, the price was attractive, leaving me more cash free for the changes I had in mind. There wouldn't be much room for a work space, but all I really needed was a laptop computer, and my MacBook Air was pretty small.

When I stepped outside onto the deck, it was on the tip of my tongue to say "I'll take it," when I looked across the water and spotted a huge boat with a for sale sign in the window. I pointed it out to the broker and asked, "What's the story on that one?"

"That's a 57 foot Grand Banks Europa, one of only three of that hull design ever made. It's a beauty, isn't it?

"Why haven't we looked at that one?"

He looked uncomfortable. "It's a lot more than you said was in your budget, and it's also 30 years old. I know you'd said you didn't want anything over 20."

I really needed to know. "How much over my budget?"

The broker cleared his throat and said, "The owner is asking $300,000."

Wow. That was more than twice what I planned on spending. But it didn't hurt to look. He had a key, so we drove the several blocks it took to get to the other side of the canal, parked and walked to the dock.

The boat looked pretty amazing from the outside, but when I stepped into the main salon, I knew I was hooked. It had been beautifully restored, and the teak and mahogany interior was gleaming. The master cabin had a king-size bed, the shower was tiled and big enough for two, and the space in the wood paneled salon would allow me to display a large selection of the books I'd collected over the years.

18

The boat also had a motivated seller. He'd bought the WanderLust seven years earlier, just before the Great Recession, and spent much of his savings to redo it from top to bottom. It was the project that kept him going, but it also made him take his attention off his investment business, which shriveled up without him noticing, until he was broke and in debt. Selling the boat became his only option.

The price would leave me little in the way of reserves, but the estate income should keep me solvent. The broker handled the negotiations with the owner, and with an updated survey of the boat's condition already complete, by the second day in Florida I was the proud owner of a boat. Dotty's house in Georgia had sold to the first couple who looked at it, and after a short wait I was able to take possession of my new home on the water.

I hired a charter captain to pilot the boat to the West Coast side of Florida on the Gulf of Mexico, and quickly realized what a good investment that was. My experience running a boat was limited to small runabouts, and the Grand Banks was pretty intimidating.

At 57 feet, standing on the flybridge felt like trying to drive a house from the roof. Not as easy as it sounds. The captain taught me the basics of navigation, and every day we explored the area from Marco Island to Naples, Venice to Sarasota, looking for the place that would be home base. Bradenton seemed like an appealing area to me, and I started looking around for a marina that was liveaboard friendly. By this time I'd docked the boat at least a dozen times, and Captain Jim declared me trained enough to get by.

"You're doing pretty good at docking, Will, and I've shown you all of the systems maintenance that's required to keep the WanderLust running smoothly. You don't really need my help anymore."

I couldn't argue, so I put in at the Bradenton Yacht Club, called a cab to run him over to the car rental office, and set back out to find a berth for my new home. It was then that I met Sandrine "Sandy" St. Martin as I checked out her little marina on the Dolphin River. She steered me to the larger Sailfin Point Marina, and our friendship was born. Now it looked like her ship had come in with the riverfront development, but I had my doubts.

Unfortunately, I'd soon be proven right.

Chapter Four

Captain Rick had stopped by The WanderLust for a beer as promised, and I got us both a frosty bottle from my cold-plate fridge in the galley. I handed the chilled Red Stripe to him and got right to the point.

"So, Rick, what do you think about this big development they plan to build on the Dolphin River?"

"Looks pretty damn fancy to me. I'm guessing there won't be anyplace there that I can afford to eat, and there sure won't be a bait shack there anymore." He looked disgusted and said, "That's what they call progress I guess."

"I imagine the city government is looking forward to the big tax windfall a place like that will bring," I said. "It's the people who are pushed out that pay the price though."

"Yep, that's the truth. I'm guessing your friend Sandy will be one of the ones who gets the short end of the stick."

"I was afraid of that. Have you heard something about it?"

Rick took a big swallow of his beer. "I've got a buddy on the surveying crew for the project, and they've got drawings that haven't been made public yet. He said there was a big park shown where the marina, the bait shack and the diner were. Doesn't look to me like your friend's marina is gonna be staying."

"I suppose I shouldn't be surprised, but it's difficult to believe they never even told her about the plans until it was announced today."

He gave a bitter laugh. "Less time for her to make a stink or try to fight it. I'll bet this thing has been in the works for years."

"Have you heard anything else about it?"

"Well, it's not exactly part of the project, but I've heard that snake Mardy Jackson has been buying up houses all over the place. Anything within a couple of miles of the river front. People thought he was nuts, some of the old shacks he's paid good money for, but now it looks pretty smart. Guess he was in the know on the new development."

Jackson was a much less reputable property developer than the ones who were building the RiverWalk complex, and I wondered how he'd found an in with them. It would be one more thread to pull out of the knot.

I sighed and said, "There's so much money behind this thing, it's pretty sure to happen. I'll do my best to help Sandy, but I'm not hopeful."

His eyes gleamed. "Somebody is dirty in this whole thing,

I'd bet my boat on it." That was a big statement from Captain Rick. His trawler, The Waxing Gibbous, was not only his home but his pride and joy. He'd bought the 42 foot Grand Banks in Maryland fifteen years earlier, driven it 1,300 miles down the IntraCoastal Waterway to Sarasota, and spent a year refurbishing it before moving it to SailFin Point. If he'd make even a rhetorical bet on it, he felt pretty sure of himself.

"I wouldn't bet against you. I think someone is dirty in this thing too. Maybe if I can find out who, there's a chance to salvage something for Sandy."

We toasted that thought with our Red Stripes, but we knew the odds against us were high.

§

When Sandy arrived at my boat for dinner, I had a bottle of Chardonnay chilled and waiting on the rear deck. I saw her stomping down the dock towards my boat, her sandy blonde hair hanging as she held her head down, muttering to herself. This did not look good.

She climbed aboard without asking, an unusual breach of boating etiquette for her, and nearly exploded.

"Bastards! Damn sorry-assed thieving bastards!"

"Hey, Sandy, calm down, what's happening?"

"I called the developer, Dick Richmond at Dolphin River Partners, and he said they had NO plans for my property, but that I should speak to the city manager about it. When I did, the guy apologized and said I should have received a letter already, that he could check and find out why I hadn't." She gulped a healthy portion of her wine. "The city wants to bulldoze my marina and

build a fancy staircase to the River Walk. A staircase! *Merde!*"
She shook her head, and I couldn't blame her for being upset.

"I bought the marina when that area was in the toilet, and now that it's going to be something special, they want to kick me out. Can they really do that?"

She wasn't going to like my answer. "Sandy, they use something called 'Eminent Domain', which means they take your property to use it for the public good. In the past it was mostly applied to road projects, building courthouses and jails, that sort of thing, but in recent years developers all across the country have convinced city governments to force people off of their land so that the developers can make a big profit."

"But that's just not right!" she exploded. "I thought America was supposed to be the land of individual rights? How can they take away my marina and call THAT freedom?"

I didn't blame her for being angry, but in my newspaper reporting experience I'd covered dozens of cases like hers. The little guy rarely won, and the best you could hope for was to tie the value of your property to the enhanced value that the new development would bring. Getting a fair price was at least better than nothing.

"I've worked so hard to make a go of this. The bank has been after me for months, the place is falling apart, but I've never been willing to give up." Tears were running down her cheeks.

"Someone came by a few months ago to ask if I would consider selling, and I threw them out. Now I know why they were there. The city and the developer are trying to screw me out of my business and my home."

24

"Sandy, I wish I could tell you that everything will be OK, but eminent domain cases are tough to fight. I can help you find a good lawyer if you like."

"I can barely keep the lights turned on, there's no way I could afford a lawyer."

"That's something I could do for you if you'd let me." She knew a little about my inheritance, and it was obvious that I wasn't hurting for money.

"I couldn't let you do that, Will. I saved for years to buy this business, and the loan from my parents was what finally made it possible. I wouldn't take any more money from them when things got *difficile*. I certainly can't take money from you."

It was the response I expected, but I'd had to try. "Without a lawyer the only question will be how much they'll pay you for the marina. There's no way out if you don't challenge it in court."

Standing to pour more wine into her glass, I was surprised when Sandy stood, took the bottle from my hands, set it down and put her arms around me. "Giving up my dream is a bitter pill. Will you hold me tonight?"

She felt wonderful in my arms, and I was almost afraid to move and break the spell. I couldn't take advantage of her emotions though. "You're upset right now. Maybe this isn't the best time to make that decision." Even as I said the words, I wanted to bite my tongue.

"Don't worry, *mon cheri,* this isn't going to change our relationship. I don't want to be alone tonight. I want to forget about the marina and greedy developers. Let's enjoy each other aboard your beautiful boat."

I had misgivings, but it was the classic "Offer I couldn't refuse", and so I didn't.

She put her lips on mine in a lingering kiss, and I could feel her nipples stiffen through her thin sundress. I was stiffening as well, but didn't want to rush things. This had been a long time coming, and I wanted the moment to last. We kissed on the deck of the WanderLust for what seemed like hours, but was really just minutes. Then we picked up our wine glasses, and I took her hand to lead her to my cabin below.

My life since the divorce hadn't exactly been chaste, but there had been no one special to me since then. I didn't know where this was going, but I knew it would be more than empty sex. In the cabin we lit a candle, sipped our wine, and I took her in my arms again, feeling the electricity of her touch as she ran her hands across my back while our tongues danced together. She tired of waiting on me, and began removing my clothes. Ever the gentleman, I helped her off with her own.

She was beautiful in the candlelight and I told her so. There wasn't much more conversation, as we were both too enthralled with each other's bodies for talk. We kissed, we touched, and we made love on my bed. She was the first to share it with me since I'd moved aboard.

We lay in each other's arms afterwards, and I had to tell her. "Sandy, we'll go tomorrow and get to the bottom of this thing. There has to be something we can do. Don't give up yet."

She pulled me tightly against her and said, "Shhh, not tonight, *mon amour*. There will be time to deal with that tomorrow."

I lay in the bed with her, but sleep wouldn't come easy. I wanted to be her knight in shining armor, rescuing her from the greedy ones who wanted to take her livelihood away. Whatever it took, I'd do my best to help her, but the old saying "You can't fight City Hall" became a truism for a reason. Courts rarely side with individuals over what is seen as "The greater good," and the riverfront project would certainly be a boon for the area and for the tax base.

As I held Sandy in my arms, one thought kept me from sleep. Someone, somewhere, had bent the rules to make the River Walk development happen.

Chapter Five

The next morning was less awkward than I expected. I woke to the smell of coffee, and found Sandy in the galley making scrambled eggs and wearing nothing but a pair of silky panties.

"Good morning mister sleepyhead. I thought I'd wait until breakfast was ready to wake you."

I put my arms around her and said, "If you'd come in to wake me dressed like that we might have never gotten out of bed."

She gave me a playful swat. "If it bothers you I'll get dressed." She was smiling when she said it, so I knew she was not annoyed.

"I'd be more upset if you put clothes on." I sat in the booth with a cup of coffee, and watched as she scooped the eggs onto two plates and brought them to the table. She sat across from me, drank from her mug and began eating. She didn't seem to need conversation, and I was enjoying her company just fine without it. When we'd both finished, she pushed her plate aside and looked up at me.

"I'm sorry I was so upset last night. That was not the way to invite you into bed with me." She was biting her lip as she said it.

I took her hand and said, "Don't worry about it. I wanted to be there for you, and I certainly enjoyed it." I paused, then added, "If you really don't want this to change our relationship though, you'll have to start wearing clothes. I can't be responsible if you don't."

She smiled at me. "What I meant about not changing our relationship was to have no obligations. As long as we have fun being together this way, we can enjoy each other."

Well, that was certainly another great offer.

I took her hand and said, "I still want to help with this River Walk thing."

A shadow came over her face. "I have to get back to the marina this morning. I left Enrique in charge, and he doesn't know how to run the cash register very well. I hope I haven't lost too many sales this morning."

I knew she was trying to avoid facing the reality of losing her marina, but the sooner I got to the bottom of this, the better. "If you like, I can do a little checking on things for you."

She put her arms around me and said, "Will, you are so good to me. If it makes you happy to look into it, that's OK with me. But don't spend your money on a lawyer."

"I won't, I'll just see what I can find out on my own. All

those years investigating stories for the newspaper ought to be good for something."

Soon she was on her way to check on things at the marina, and I sat down to make a list of people to talk to.

Dick Richmond at Dolphin River Partners

Bill Bixler, the City Manager of Dolphin River

Curt Stoneham, The head of the City Planners office

Mayor Richard "Blackie" Ferguson

Mardy Jackson, shady developer

Maybe among the five of them, I could find out why they were trying to destroy Sandy's livelihood, along with the diner and the bait shack next to her.

§

I made a few phone calls, starting with the local paper. I'd crossed paths with Ben Carlson, one of the city desk reporters at The Bradenton Journal, when I'd reported on a hurricane a few years back. While we weren't exactly buddies, I felt like I knew him well enough to pick his brain a little.

"Ben, this is Will Harper, I was with the newspaper in Georgia and you guys let me work out of your office during the last big hurricane?"

"Hey, Will, good to hear from you. I thought I heard a 'was' in there, have you moved to another paper, or gotten smart and quit this racket?"

I laughed, and said, "I took the smart route. It was only a matter of time before my job went away with the rest of the industry."

He sighed. "Boy, isn't that the truth. Most of my friends at papers across the country have lost their jobs, and they are all going into public relations or starting their own businesses. What are you up to these days?"

"Believe it or not, I'm semi-retired, and living in Dolphin River, not far from you."

"No shit? How'd you manage that, did you win the lottery or something?" He knew I hadn't made enough as a reporter to retire while still in my thirties.
"Nothing quite that exciting. I had a relative die and leave me her house and a few investments, enough to give me an income while I try my hand at fiction writing."

"Lucky dog! I'll probably have to work at something until I die. I've got fifteen years in at this paper, but I need to make twenty five for a decent pension check. The likelihood of my job lasting ten more years is not looking good. They want to replace all of the older guys like me with kids fresh out of journalism school, and pay them half of what they pay us. You know how it is these days."

We commiserated about the sad state of newspapers for a few more minutes, and then I told him why I'd called. "Listen, Ben, how much do you know about the River Walk project planned for Dolphin River?"

"Only what they've officially released about it," he answered. There have been rumors about a big development in the area for years, but no one's been able to pin down a location until now. It's kind of like when the Disney folks were buying up land for Disney World, all of the developers were so tight lipped you'd have thought it was a national security issue. They didn't want to pay inflated prices for the land, so they used a bunch of straw buyers. Sounds like the Dolphin River guys took the same approach, just on a smaller scale." He paused, and said, "What's your interest in this thing?"

"Personal, not professional. A friend of mine owns the marina in the middle of the River Walk project, and she's been told that they are taking her land and two other pieces to build a public access staircase. Eminent domain, so she's being told she has no say in the matter."

Sounding disgusted, Ben said, "Eminent domain! That's nothing more than a license for government theft of private property these days. Anytime a wealthy developer wants to take something that a property owner doesn't want to part with, they make a public project out of it and take it anyway. The developers get rich, and the landowners get screwed."

"Yeah, that's pretty much the case here. They haven't told her how much they will offer her yet, but you can bet it won't be enough to make her give up her livelihood. This marina is all she has, and if it could be a part of the new development she'd make a mint. They want to keep all the money for themselves, though."

"Listen, Will, I'll help in any way I can, but the newspaper's owner are big civic boosters, and they think this thing is great. Some of them probably have an investment stake too. Don't expect our paper to write any expose´s about it."

"I know how that goes, I was hoping that you could just let me know who the power brokers are behind this thing. I plan to dig around a little and see what I can find. I do a little freelance writing for some Florida travel magazines, so I might use that as a cover. Tell them I'm writing a story about the project."

"Sounds good, let me know what I can do. Give me your email, and I'll send you what I have on it."

We said our goodbyes, and promised to keep in touch. Journalism had always been something of a fraternity, and it was sad to see it crumbling, replaced by opinionated bloggers and TV networks featuring talking heads who screamed at each other. What a waste.

§

I decided to start at the top of my list, and called to make an appointment with the head of Dolphin River Partners. With the newly announced project they were looking for publicity, and I was quickly transferred to a PR person who made me an appointment for later that morning. I'd called *Florida Waterways* magazine and arranged to send them a spec story on the project, so my cover was in place. They weren't obligated to buy it and I wasn't contracted to write it, but it gave my phone calls a touch of legitimacy.

Dick Richmond ushered me into his office, and was quick to start his sales pitch. "Mr. Harper, glad you could come by! *Florida Waterways* is one of my favorite magazines, and I'm pleased you want to do a story on our project."

He gestured towards two plush chairs in front of his desk, and we sat as I started my own spiel. "Mr. Richmond, thanks for seeing me. You know our magazine does a lot of environmental reporting, and I'd like to start with the angle of the River Walk project's impact on the locals."

"Call me Dick, please. Well, first of all, we predict that when the construction is complete, it will attract $10 million annually in sales to the local economy. With tourists spending money on hotels, restaurants and shopping, it will be a real boon to the area. Then there are the tax benefits. The increase in the tax base will raise the county's annual tax collection by as much as twenty per cent over the next decade."

I tried to start slowly. "Yes, but Dick, don't the city and county have to make a substantial investment up front to provide utilities and roads for the project?"

"That's true, but you have to spend money to make money you know, Will. Is it OK if I call you Will?"

"Sure. But back to my question, the county is building the utilities and roads, but isn't the city going to have to make a large investment in the grounds, landscaping all of the roads and entryways?" Then I slipped in my real question. "And what about the public staircase and park on the river front? With several businesses being displaced, won't that be a big upfront cost?"

He looked a little uncomfortable, and said, "The park is a pretty big investment by the city, sure, but the benefits to the public are worth it. It will be a place for the citizens to gather, their access to the river in the middle of the development." He leaned back and looked satisfied with his characterization of things. "It will be a beautiful place."

I didn't let him off the hook. "But isn't it a major amenity to the River Walk development? Seems like the taxpayers are helping your company make a lot of money by building a park and the staircase. The citizens have free access to the waterfront already."

"Now, Will, you're looking at this the wrong way. The reason the city wanted to get involved is because this will benefit *everyone*!"

Time for a zinger. "Not everyone. How about the marina, bait shack and diner that are being forced out? How does that benefit them?"

Now he had that 'deer in the headlights' look. "Uh, Mr. Harper, I'm sure they will be compensated fairly for their properties. Sometimes older, more run-down businesses need to go to make way for progress." He was ready to cut this off. "Perhaps you should talk to the city officials who decided to build this park. It is, after all, a public project, and not strictly part of our development."

"Who designed it, your firm or the city?"

Richmond squirmed in his chair. "Well of course, we worked with the city to make sure it was well integrated into our architectural plans, but I really think you should ask the mayor about that."

He looked at his watch, and said, "I have another meeting now, thanks for stopping by." Standing, he shook my hand and said "Look, this project is going to put Dolphin River on the map. Surely you see that it's a good thing?"

"Actually, I do, but it seems that it's a lot better for you than it is for the people losing their businesses."

He had no answer for that, and I turned and walked out of

his office. I could tell this wasn't the kind of publicity he had in mind.

Chapter Six

Taking the developer's advice, I made my next stop at city hall. I didn't have an appointment, but I knew that Mayor Blackie Ferguson usually worked in his office in the morning, making the rounds of public appearances and ribbon cuttings later in the day before spending the evenings at his used car lot, Blackie's Bargain Rides. I wanted to catch him off guard, so I arrived mid-morning.

Dawn, his secretary said he was on the phone, but should be able to see me momentarily. A few minutes later, his door opened and he said, "Mr. Harper, come on in!"

That was odd, since she hadn't given him my name when I came in. I shook his hand as I walked into his office, and asked him about it. "Were you expecting me?"

"Yes, I just got off the phone with Dick Richmond at Dolphin River Partners. He said you'd be stopping by."

"Looks like news travels fast."

He laughed and said, "Being a journalist, you should know that." He sat, pulled his sleeves up, and leaned in towards me to give the conversation an illusion of privacy. "Dick tells me that you seem to have the wrong idea about our participation in the River Walk project."

I decided to play dumb. "Oh, and how is that?"

"He got the impression that you thought we weren't being fair to the businesses being displaced by the park and staircase."

Well, at least he was direct. "Losing their businesses so the developer can have a fancy park in the middle of a very profitable complex hardly seems fair to me."

The mayor turned his dark, intense eyes on me, the source, along with his thick head of black hair, of his nick-name. "Mr. Harper, sometimes to benefit the whole city I have to make decisions that might not suit a few people. Those businesses are run down and out of date. They wouldn't fit into a beautiful development like the River Walk, and so they have to go. I assure you, they will be compensated for their loss."

"Does that mean, Mr. Mayor, that the property owners will be reimbursed for the lost business? If they were included in the property development, it could come to quite a bit of money they would stand to earn. Will you make up for that loss?"

Now he just looked irritated. "MISTER Harper, as the mayor, I have to be fiscally accountable. We'll certainly pay the property owners for the current value of their land and buildings, but it's not the responsibility of our small city to pay them for something they might have earned in the future. Surely you can understand that?"

"I'm afraid I understand full well," I said. "The developers will make a mint, the city tax rolls will grow, and those little businesses will just be gone."

He harrumphed, and said, "You are taking this all wrong. We're talking about the greater good here."

"When will the property owners receive the city's offer for their businesses?"

"The city manager has been working on those figures, but as I said, the compensation is for the land and buildings, not for whatever businesses they may be running in them."

He stood and said, "Mr. Harper, this project is happening, and I would suggest that you don't try to interfere with it. It's important to the city."

That sounded vaguely threatening, but I made my way out of his office without replying. It was beginning to look like a steamroller was heading for Sandy's marina, and it wasn't going to be pretty.

§

I went to the office of City Manger Bill Bixler, but wasn't surprised to be told he was out on city business. I'm sure he'd been warned to avoid talking to me, and I got the same response when I stopped by the City Planner's office. The curtain was being pulled closed on the project they'd been so eager to publicize, but that didn't mean it would slow anything, just that it would be harder for me to get any information.

I decided to try Mardy Jackson next, since he wasn't directly involved with the developers or the city. I drove to his office on the edge of the business district, located in a slightly seedy-looking office building that reminded me of a motel from the 1960's. It was close to lunch time, and when I walked into his small office suite, the secretary's desk was vacant. The office door was open, and a voice called through it.

"Hey Blackie, that you? Come on in."

I walked in, introduced myself, and said, "Were you expecting the mayor?"

He covered himself smoothly. "No, Blackie is an old high school buddy, Jim Williams is his real name, but we called him Blackie cause he was always losing fights and getting black eyes. What can I do for you?" He quickly texted a message to someone, and I wondered if the mayor was the one being warned of my presence.

"I understand you've been buying quite a lot of property near the new River Walk development."

"Well, son, I'm always buying and selling property and buildings, it's what I do for a living."

"Yes, but I understand that an awful lot of your purchases over the last six months have been ones that will be the most profitable now that the River Walk project is public. Who tipped you off about the project?"

Jackson looked indignant, and said "Now listen here, nobody tipped me off about anything. I've been doing this a long time, and I knew that something good would happen on the river front eventually. Buying when I did was a lucky guess." He leaned back in his chair and smiled, and I didn't believe a word he'd said.

"Not so lucky for the folks who sold out. They'd have gotten a lot higher price once the River Walk was announced. Homes within walking distance would go at a premium," I said.

"Mr. Harper, there are winners and losers in the real estate business, and I try to always be a winner."

Now *that* I believed. "If you had inside information, that could be seen as conspiracy to defraud." I wasn't sure if that was true in a legal sense, but he could certainly find himself in lawsuits from unhappy sellers.

Now he was angry. "I told you I did not have anything of the sort. This interview is over, and if you ever print anything that says I profited off insider information, I'll sue you for slander." He stood up, gestured at the door, and said, "Good day."

I left without arguing, but I knew I had hit a nerve. Now I had to find out who was the source of his information about the project. I'm betting there had been payoffs involved, and that was bribing a public official. Definitely a crime, and one that could put him behind bars.

§

It was now early afternoon, and I stopped at a little pub near city hall for a late lunch. After my beer and burger arrived, my eyes began to adjust to the dim light in the place, and I saw that I was not alone. In a booth near the front sat City Planner Curt Stoneham, deep in conversation with someone I didn't recognize. The other man was a rough-looking guy, wearing a sleeveless tee with a flaming skull on it, tattoos covering his arms. Somehow this didn't look like official business.

No one had come in since I'd arrived, so it meant they had

been meeting before I got there, and the sideways looks that Stoneham cast towards me suggested that he wasn't happy I'd seen them together. After a few more minutes, he got up and left the bar, going out the door without a backward glance. The tough guy stayed, staring at me as he finished his beer. I thought for a minute he was coming over to talk to me when he stood up and stared some more, but he tossed a few bills on the table and walked out the door.

I had to wonder where he fit in all this.

After finishing my burger and a second beer, I walked out to my car. One of my little splurges with Aunt Dotty's inheritance had been a black, BMW Z4, complete with a retractable hardtop. I'd bought it used from a snowbird who'd only put 18,000 miles on it in four years, and it had been a bargain. Not the most practical vehicle for someone living on a boat, but who said I needed to be practical?

When I looked at my car, I was pissed to see the tough guy from the pub leaning on my fender. He watched me approach, and when I got close, I told him "Please get off of my car. Black paint scratches easily." I didn't raise my voice, but I wasn't going to back down either.

He made a big show of standing up and brushing off the fender, saying, "Why, excuse me, I had no idea this was your car."

I waited to see what he wanted, but he was silent. I got in the car, put the top down as he watched, and then I drove away. Maybe the point was to get my attention, and he'd done that. His involvement with the city planner seemed unlikely, and I wanted to know what their connection was. Maybe I should just ask.

Driving back to city hall, I went to Curt Stoneham's office, and asked to see him. There was a fill-in receptionist while the regular one was at lunch, and she apparently hadn't been warned to tell me that he wasn't in, so she called him to announce me.

"Mr. Stoneham, there's a Will Harper here to see you. Yes, he's standing right here. I'm sorry, no one told me. OK, I'll send him back." She pointed down the hallway towards his office, and said, "He'll see you now." She leaned in and whispered "But I don't think he likes you."

I grinned and said, "What, a friendly guy like me?"

She smiled back, and I started down the hall. His door was ajar, and I tapped on it as I walked in. "Mr. Stoneham? Will Harper from *Florida Waterways* magazine. I'm doing a story on the environmental and social impact of the River Walk project."

He shook my hand, and said, "I've only got a few minutes free. What can I do for you?"

"Like I said, I'm writing a story about the impact of the development, and I assume the City Planner's office had a lot of input." I let the sentence hang there.

After a pause, he said, "Yes, I suppose that's right."

I decided to get straight to the point. "So, was it your department that recommended that a park and staircase be built where the marina, diner and bait shack are currently located?"

He looked like he was starting to sweat. "We worked closely with the mayor's office and with Dolphin River Partners to decide how best to make the project easily accessible to the public, and that was the solution we came up with. If you'll look at the drawings, I think you'll see that it makes a lot of sense to put it there." He gestured at the drawing on the wall, the park and the staircase clearly shown. Those details had been left out of the drawing that the newspaper had published.

"And what about the businesses that are being forced out to make way for it?"

"I wouldn't say they are being forced out. They will be compensated for their land." I noticed he didn't say 'and businesses.'

"And when will they be told what the city is offering them as compensation? Seems like that would have been the first thing that was done, to avoid bad publicity. Forcing people off of their land isn't usually a popular thing to do."

"Not that it's really any of your business, Mr. Harper, but those letters are going out this afternoon. I'm sure everyone will agree that the offers are very fair."

Nothing I'd heard so far made me think that would be true. I decided I'd better plan on being with Sandy when the mail arrived.

Chapter Seven

The next day I dropped by the marina to visit Sandy, not sure of how she would take the news that things weren't looking promising for her waterfront business. Being the bearer of bad news isn't a fun task in the best of circumstances, and our personal involvement wasn't going to make it any easier.

Sandy was outside repairing a leaky waterline that ran to one set of boat slips when she spotted me walking down the dock.

"Will, I didn't know you were coming to see me." She wiped the perspiration from her face with a towel before leaning over for a welcome kiss.

"I wanted to give you an update on what I've found out so far. I have some pretty strong suspicions that this staircase plan wasn't handled properly, but that doesn't mean it will be easy to stop," I told her.

"*Mon ami*, I have faith in you. I know you can work miracles when you set your mind to it." She was looking at me adoringly, and I hated to burst her bubble.

"Sandy, don't get your hopes up. Having suspicions and proving them are two different things, and even if I can prove somebody broke the law, it doesn't mean the eminent domain case will go away. The best I can promise is to put pressure on them to give you a fair price."

She looked crestfallen at my statement. "Is there no way to save this marina? Are you really going to let those greedy bastards take it away from me?"

"Hey, I'm doing everything I can to help you. I just don't want you to get your heart set on beating the city and keeping the business here. I've seen it go the other way too many times. Please don't blame me because it's unfair. I want to fix this for you, but I really don't know if it's possible."

With a sad expression, she began putting her tools away. "I don't know why I should try to repair things around here if I'm going to lose it anyway."

I put a hand under her chin to tilt her face up to me. "Sandy, don't give up yet. I haven't, OK?"

A tear ran down her cheek, and she looked away before going back to packing up.

This was going as badly as I feared it might, and I knew it could get worse. It did when the mail arrived a few minutes later.

"Son of a beetch!" she screamed as she held the letter containing the city's offer for her marina. "They are insane!"

I took the letter from her and looked at the numbers.

Four hundred thousand dollars for the land and building. Even worse than I expected.

"I owe the bank over $370,000, and I put $200,000 down on it from my parents when I bought it. Are they mad? There is no way I could settle for this. What are they trying to do to me?"

"It's a first offer, and most eminent domain cases start by offering what they would like to pay for it, not what they're willing to spend. Don't panic yet."

"But Will, I won't only be broke and unemployed, I'll owe my parents nearly $200,000 with no way to pay it back! I can't do that to them."

She had a wild look on her face, and I tried to calm her down. "Sandy, I promise this will get better. We'll publicize what the city is trying to do to you and the other two businesses in the way of their damn staircase. The city and the developers won't like that at all. We need time for the pressure on them to build."

"There is no time. The city says they want an answer within thirty days."

I grinned and said, "Oh, we'll give them an answer, but they won't like it much."

It was time to go to plan B.

"I know a great attorney in Atlanta who owes me a big favor. I kept a client of his out of a story that would have damaged his business, and he said he'd be glad to help me any time."

"Please, Will, I don't want to take money from you. I can't afford a lawyer."

"He can do most of this by mail, and he hates to see a

small business screwed by corrupt politics. I'll bet he'll love this case."

She looked worried, but said, "As long as it's not costing you money. Owing my parents is bad enough."

I took her in my arms. "Sandy, I don't know how much I can do to help, but this is one thing I can do. We have to at least try. Let me give him a call."

§

Walter Lord was a big name in Atlanta legal circles, but he always treated me like an old college buddy.

"Will, how's life on the boat! I couldn't believe it when you quit that crummy newspaper to go sailing."

I laughed and said, "It's not a sailboat, it's a trawler, and life is great for me. I'm shocked at how little I miss the news business." I paused and added, "There is something I need your help with though."

"Anything, you've got it. I haven't forgotten what you did for Jim when you kept his business out of that story on contractor fraud."

"Listen, Walter, I told you that I kept him out because it was a few of his employees that were scamming people. He had nothing to do with it, and it wouldn't have been fair to destroy his business that way."

"Still, you didn't have to do it. I've known plenty of reporters who don't care about messing up peoples lives, and we were both grateful you weren't one of them."

"I was glad to help."

"So how can I help you now, Will?"

"A friend of mine owns a small marina here in Dolphin River, and the city is taking it and two other properties through eminent domain to build a park and a staircase to the riverfront. It sits right in the middle of a $65 million dollar private development, and it sure looks like a gift to the developer from the city."

"You know I'll help how ever I can, Will, but eminent domain cases are tough. The courts usually side with the municipalities if there's even a half-way decent reason to take the property."

"I've tried to tell my friend Sandy that, but she wants to fight it. The worst part is that they are offering a ridiculously low price to buy the property. $400,000 is the opening offer."

"Good grief, that's a low price for *any* marina, what with the environmental hurdles it takes to start a new one."

"I know, Walter, but they seem to think they have a strong case."

"Seems like I heard a *she* in that first statement, how close a friend is this Sandy?" I could almost see his grin over the phone.

"Well, we've been friends for awhile, but it only moved into something else a few weeks ago. She's a great person who has put her life savings into this business, and it sucks that the city can just take it from her right when it could become a bonanza, sitting in the middle of the new development. I really hate it for her."

"OK, don't promise her anything, but I'll see what can be done. At the very least we should get a much better price than the pittance they've offered so far."

"I really appreciate this. Let me know what it costs, and I'll be glad to cover your fees."

He laughed and said, "Normally I'd say you can't afford me, but the rumor going around is that you hit the jackpot. None the less, I'll consider this repayment of a debt."

"At least let me pay for any expenses, OK?"

"That's a deal. You can start by emailing everything you have on the situation, including who the players are and what's happened so far. With your background, that should be an easy task."

"I've actually been doing a little investigating myself. Looks to me like it's a good old boy network where the politicians and the developers all get rich at the expense of the landowners."

"Nothing new about that, I'm afraid. If you can find out whether some of the city employees made money on this deal, that will ratchet up the pressure on them to settle. Keep me posted on what you learn."

"Thanks, Walter, I owe you one."

"No you don't, but this will get us back to even. Who knows, I may need a favor from you some day."

"If you ever want a weekend on a beautiful boat, I know just the place. I'll even buy the beer."

We said our goodbyes, and I called Sandy to tell her that my friend would be helping us out.

"Will, do you think he might be able to save my marina?"

"He thought the same thing I did, Sandy. Stopping the

eminent domain case is a long shot. But we can at least get you a better price. Listen, why don't you come over to my boat tonight? I'll grill some steaks, and I have wine in the cabinet. You can try to forget all of this for at least one night."

"I'm afraid I would be very poor company."

"Just come over, I'll take care of the rest."

§

The steaks were great, we drank two bottles of wine, and by midnight we were wrapped around each other in my bed, trying to catch our breath after a wild lovemaking session that felt tinged with desperation. Now I was struggling to stay awake, but she was holding me tightly. Somehow I knew she was thinking of the marina.

"Will?"

"Hmmm?"

"What if I have to go away?"

That woke me up. "Why would you have to leave?"

"If I lose the marina, I won't be able to stay in the U.S. My visa is for running a business here."

Damn. I hadn't thought of that.

"Don't worry about that now. We're still fighting this."

She pulled me closer still, and said, "I was just getting used to this. I'm not ready to lose you."

I kissed the top of her head, and said, "I'm getting pretty used to this myself. Lets face this one day at a time, OK?"

She nodded an agreement, tucked her head into my chest, and dozed off. I lay there and watched her beautiful breasts rise and fall with her breathing, marveling at my good fortune in finding Sandrine. We seemed so good together. Would the City of Dolphin River destroy her business and our budding relationship all at once?

Not if I could stop them.

Chapter Eight

When I woke the next morning, my bed was empty. Sandy was already gone. At least she'd left a note, telling me that she had to get back to the marina for her early morning customers, and I couldn't argue with that. Fishermen get started before dawn, and I knew it was important for her to be sure the gas pumps were running to get them on their way.

She'd made a pot of coffee before leaving, and I poured myself a cup and went on deck to admire the sunny morning. Living on the water in Florida is as close to a tropical lifestyle as you can get in the continental United States, and I tried to make the most of it every morning.

SailFin Point Marina where I keep my boat is a friendly place, and I lifted my coffee cup in greeting to several of my neighbors as they walked down the docks. Just when I was about to go in for a refill, I spotted Captain Rick as he walked down from his boat at the other end of the dock that we both lived on.

"Morning Rick" I called to him. "Had your coffee yet?"

"I've had plenty thanks, I've been up since six a.m. Got a minute?"

"Sure, come aboard." He climbed on deck and joined me on the flybridge. "What's up?"

He had a look that told me there was news, and I waited patiently for him to get around to spilling it.

"You know that thing with the Dolphin River Marina we talked about. The one where they were trying to take it away from that nice girl, Sandy?" He knew I did, but he got to the point slowly sometimes.

"Yes, what about it?"

"Well, I've been asking around a little, just among my friends, you know. Seems to be kind of an open secret that the mayor and some of the other folks in city government have done a little investing in that fancy new development. Maybe they even got cut in at what you might say was a 'special price' on the deal."

"I can't say I'm surprised," I told him. "Proving it might be tough though."

"Yep, there's lot's of shell corporations involved, and I'll bet tracking the ownership of all that would be a mess." Rick still had a little grin on his grizzled face, and I had a feeling there was more to this.

"What else aren't you telling me, Rick?"

"Oh, just that there's this fella, way down on the totem pole in the planning department, and he's not too happy with what's going on with that development."

Now it was getting interesting. "How so?"

"He was on the team that did the planning work for the city on how to incorporate the new development into the existing riverfront, and they started out by assuming that the marina, the bait shop and the diner would stay. It was presented to the head of the planning department, and he overruled them, told them to design a park and riverfront access where those buildings were. Said the developer wanted them gone."

"I'm surprised Curt Stoneham would be so candid with his staff about the developer interfering like that, Rick. That seems risky."

"Nah, they're all afraid of him and the mayor. If you don't play along, you lose your job real quick."

"So who is the one in the planning office who's unhappy about it? Is he willing to be a whistle blower on this?"

"Not so much. But he told his girlfriend, who told her mother, and she is sleeping with my friend Jim, who lives over on dock nine, and when I started asking around, he told me. I promised him I'd keep it quiet."

"Rick, you know I need to talk to this guy, right?"

He grinned and said, "I told Jim that I'd just tell you." He reached in his pocket and pulled out a folded piece of paper. "His name is Andy Mays. Here's his name and cell phone number. You might want to wait until he's off work to call him, though."

"Rick, you are a miracle worker. This could be just the thing we need to stop them from taking Sandy's marina. I'll call him tonight."

"Don't expect Andy to be happy to hear from you. It sounds like there was some pressure on him to keep quiet about it."

"I'll try to protect him as much as I can, but this is bribery we're talking about. If the mayor and city planner are taking pieces of the development in return for giving Dolphin River Partners free rein on who stays and who gets kicked off the river front, that's a crime. If it becomes a legal matter, he may have to testify."

"Do what you can to shield him, Will. Jim's going to be pissed if his girlfriend finds out he told me about this."

I patted him on the shoulder and said "You know I'll try my best."

It might be a challenge, though.

§

It was starting out cooler than the usual steamy Florida day, so I took the morning to catch up on maintenance projects on my boat before doing anything more on Sandy's marina problem. An old saying about boats is that they are "a hole in the water into which you pour money", and it's not far from the truth. The best way to keep a boat from bleeding you dry is to take good care of it. I was determined not to let the projects get away from me.

The first chore was a sticky float switch, and it had let my bilge get half filled with dirty water before I noticed the problem. Since it wasn't coming on automatically, I'd had to run it on manual several times to keep the bilge dry, and replacing it couldn't wait any longer. It wasn't a hard job, but crawling around in the bilge was dirty, sweaty work, and I was glad when I had the new one working after only scraping my knuckles a few times.

I dove in the water off the stern in my shorts to cool off, then spent another forty-five minutes sanding some of the brightwork in preparation for a new coat of varnish. The WanderLust has a fiberglass hull, but there is a fair amount of mahogany in the rails and decorative trim, and the Florida sun bakes it to a crisp regularly. It was a months long project to get it all sanded and revarnished, and by the time I had finished the boat front to back, it would be time to start over at the other end again. Nobody said this lifestyle was easy.

It was getting hot, so I grabbed a shower in my cabin, changed into my usual tropical attire of flowered shirt and shorts, and drove the Z4 into town, stopping first at my favorite local dive for a grouper sandwich. Kevin's Crab Shack isn't fancy, but the food is delicious, and I try to eat there at least once a week. Filled and rested, it was time to get to work.

The only person from my list of people to talk to about the River Walk development who I hadn't caught up with was City Manager Bill Bixler. He'd been avoiding me, so I tried a new tactic. I paid one of the landscaping workers I spotted trimming the hedges outside city hall ten bucks to go to the city manager's office and ask the secretary if Bixler was available for a quick question. She called him to the lobby, and when he showed up, I was there waiting for him. He looked around for the landscaper, who had already made his escape, and when he spotted me instead he got a sour look on his face. I wasn't about to let him get away.

"Mr. Bixler? Hi, I'm Will Harper, I've been trying to reach you with a few questions about the city's involvement in the new River Walk development."

"I thought someone from the grounds crew was looking for me?"

"Gee, I think he left already. In the meantime, I'm here now, and I just need a few minutes of your time."

There was no graceful way to refuse, and he reluctantly said, "OK, I've got about ten minutes before my next meeting. Come to my office."

I followed him into the office suite, past the chagrined looking secretary and into his office. I'd bet she was going to get an earful after I left.

"So, Mr. Harper, what did you want to know?"

"I understand your office was responsible for coming up with the numbers for the offers on the river front properties that the city is attempting to take by eminent domain?"

A superior smile crept over his face. "Oh, Mr. Harper, I wouldn't say the city is *attempting* to take those derelict properties. Trust me, it will happen."

"Whether it happens or not, I can't believe you think the city will get all of that land for the bargain basement prices you came up with."

Now he looked indignant. "Mr. Harper, those are fair prices based on what land has sold for on the riverfront in the past. I have an obligation to the city not to overpay for properties just because the owners need the money. We have to run this like any business, with an eye on the bottom line."

"Look, Bixler, you haven't allowed anything in those prices for the businesses, just a vacant land price."

"Vacant land is what they are to the city, MISTER Harper. It will cost a fortune to tear those buildings down as it is."

"That's not a reasonable approach and you know it. Those three businesses exist because they support each other. The fishermen stop at the diner for breakfast, buy their bait at the bait shack and their gas from the marina. It's not like they can just pick up and relocate. You will be taking the livelihood of three families, and all you want to pay for is the land? That's criminal."

"Sir, I can assure you that this is all perfectly legal. I consulted with the city attorney before finalizing our offer and everything is by the book. I think we are done here, Mr. Harper. I have other work to do."

I couldn't resist a parting shot. "Don't think for a second that these folks are all going to go quietly so that your developer buddies can fatten their wallets, Bixler. I'm going to shine the light of publicity on this deal and the city won't come out looking very good. Stealing property from citizens to give to developers isn't what the government exists for. What does it say on the city motto, 'To Serve and Protect'? You're not doing either."

His face was purple as he said, "Get out. Now."

At least we both agreed *that* was a good idea.

Chapter Nine

I'd already talked to everyone in city government who could possibly shed light on the reasoning behind replacing three viable businesses on the river front with a park and a staircase. Now I needed to get Sandy's two neighbors on board with my plan to fight it.

Ron and Carol Cox had owned the Dolphin River Diner for more than fifteen years, and in that time they'd made it a staple of the slightly shabby area where it was located. It was to the right of Sandy's marina, and looked considerably better than it had when they bought it. Built out of concrete block, the way much of this part of Florida had been in the 1950's, the Coxes had added an awning, re-covered the booths with new vinyl and changed out the old fluorescent lighting for hanging light fixtures that Carol had decorated with sea shells.

The food was simple but good, and in addition to the

steady stream of traffic from the fishermen who fished the waters of the river and the nearby bay, local families filled the place most evenings, eager for their fried fish and clam strip dinners. It was a good business for Ron and Carol. They weren't getting rich, but they were making a nice living.

Now the River Walk developers and the city wanted to take it away.

It was midafternoon, between the lunch rush and the dinner crowd, and when I opened the door the bell mounted above it brought Carol out from behind the counter.

"Will, what brings you in today? It's a little late for lunch, isn't it?"

"Hi Carol. Have you and Ron got a minute to sit and talk?"

She took her apron off, grabbed her ever present glass of iced tea, lifted it up to me and said, "I've got time, but Ron is over in Bradenton picking up parts for the walk-in cooler fan. Want some tea?"

They made nice, strong, unsweetened tea, perfect for a hot day. "Sure, I'd love a glass."

She poured it over ice, and we sat at a table close to the register. We drank our tea, and she waited for me to speak first.

"Carol, I've been trying to help Sandy deal with the fallout from this eminent domain case, and I wanted to see where you and Ron were on it."

She looked like she'd bitten into something sour, and said, "Where we are is screwed, that's where we are."

I was a little taken aback by her bitterness, although in

retrospect I shouldn't have been surprised.

"Before we moved down from South Carolina, we had a nice little restaurant up there. Nothing fancy, kind of like this place. Then the city decided we were part of a 'blighted' area, and started putting the screws to us. Code violations, fire hazards, everything they could think of to shut us down. When we finally gave up, they paid us about half of what it was worth, and bulldozed the building so they could 'improve' the area. You know what's there now?"

I shook my head no as she took a sip from her tea.

"A damn empty lot. Nothing. No improvements, no new restaurants, nothing. The people who ate at our place everyday now have to walk four blocks from where they work to pay twice as much for their lunches. Some improvement."

"I can see why you're angry, Carol. This must feel like the same thing all over again."

"No, Will. This is worse. Those bastards are going to build a huge development all around us, something that could have made this little restaurant enough of a success to leave something for our grandkids. They just don't want to share any of it."

A tear slid down her cheek, and she said, "We're going to lose everything. The offer they've made will pay our bills for two or three years, and then we'll be living on social security. Do you know what it's like to be self-employed your whole life and then go on social security? We never paid ourselves much of a salary, we couldn't afford to. So the amount we'll get every month will barely keep a roof over our heads. Ron and I are probably both going to have to get jobs after they kick us out of here."

"Carol, I don't know how much I can do, but I want to help."

"That's nice of you, Will, but what can you do?" She snorted with laughter, and said, "You plan to let us come live on the boat with you?"

"I've got an attorney friend that's going to bat for Sandy on this thing, and he's willing to include the diner and the bait shack in the deal, since it's all adjoining property."

She looked sad and said, "I appreciate the gesture, honey, but we don't have any money for a lawyer. We can't afford to fight this."

"The money isn't a problem. The attorney is a friend who owes me a favor, and he's something of a crusader against government land grabs. His name is Walter Lord, and he's not making promises that he can stop the eminent domain case, but he's confident that he can at least drive up the price the city has to pay."

A glimmer of hope lit up Carol's face. "Oh, Will, that would be wonderful. If we could get enough to start some other kind of business, then I know we'd find a way to get by." She stood and leaned down and gave me a hug. "You're a good man."

"Hey, don't expect too much, but I know Walter will do his best on this. He's a bulldog when he sees a city land grab, and that's what this is."

"Will, any chance of this getting stopped is one we'll take. Ron's been so depressed since we got that letter from the city manager saying what they'll pay us, I thought he'd about given up. This should brighten his spirits."

I stood up, and said, "Thanks for the tea, Carol. I'm going over to the bait shack to talk to Bob now, since he's a part of this too."

"Good luck with him. Bob has been threatening to blow up city hall over this."

I laughed and said, "Don't worry, I'll keep my distance until I make sure he's not armed." I walked to the door, waved goodbye, and stepped into the heat. It was a short walk to the bait shack, and I hoped that the owner would be as receptive as Carol had been.

§

Bob's Bait Shack was a little rougher looking than either the marina or the diner, and I could sort of understand why the developers might want to get rid of it. It would take a little imagination, but a new facade wouldn't cost much for the small building. It was an integral part of the old river front atmosphere that I hoped wasn't going to disappear. Unfortunately, property developers weren't known for their desire to save old buildings.

When I walked in the front door, Bob was in his usual attire of grubby long sleeved denim shirt with the sleeves rolled up, a once white captains cap on his balding head. His shaggy, gray beard gave him a slight Hemingway look, but I don't think he spent a lot of time with books.

"Will, what brings you in today?" Although I wasn't a fisherman, Bob seemed to know everyone who owned a boat in a ten mile radius and he always remembered their names. I'd always wished for that skill, but it wasn't one I possessed.

"Hi Bob. Keeping busy?"

"As long as they let me stay here, I'm selling bait. I'm not leaving until the marshall drags me away."

Eviction isn't a pretty sight, and I hoped it wouldn't come to that. "That's why I'm here. I want to talk to you about the eminent domain case."

"The city wants something from an honest businessman and they just take it. Bastards."

"That seems to be the consensus around here. I guess you got an offer letter from the city manager?"

"What a joke! They want to give me $60,000 for a piece of land on the river! Those assholes spend more than that on their cars." He shook his head. "I know this building ain't much, but the bait shack has put a roof over my head and kept me fed for more than thirty years. It isn't fair that they can just steal it from me in plain sight."

"Listen, Bob, I have an attorney friend that is helping Sandy fight this thing. He suggested that the Bait Shack and the Diner be included. Are you OK with that?"

He looked down at the ground and said quietly, "I don't have any money for lawyers, Will. I barely keep the bills paid as it is."

"Money isn't an issue. Walter Lord is an old friend who owed me a favor and he's happy to do this. All you have to do is agree to let him represent you against the city, and there won't be any bills."

"Damn, that's awful nice of him, and you too, Will."

"No promises, but he feels like he'll at least get a better settlement. Stopping the eminent domain case entirely is a much longer shot, but he's going to try."

He reached over the counter and shook my hand, saying, "It's a hell of a lot more than I expected to happen. I don't want to leave this place without a fight, but I didn't even know how to. Thanks, Will."

"No problem, glad I can be of some help. I'll keep you posted on how it's going." I took my leave and went back out into the Florida heat. The boat traffic going lazily by the rustic river front buildings looked like a scene from a time gone by and I wanted to keep it from disappearing. It wouldn't be easy.

§

The day had been very productive, and I hoped the evening would be as well. I waited until six o'clock, and made the call to my potential witness, the unhappy planning department employee. He was not thrilled with my call.

"Hi, is this Andy Mays? My name is Will Harper, I'm a reporter doing a story for *Florida Waterways* magazine on the RiverWalk development, and I wanted to talk with you about it." There was silence on the phone, and at first I thought he'd hung up.

"I don't know why you're calling me. I'm just an employee in the department, you'd need to speak to the head of planning, Curt Stoneham. I can give you his number if you like."

"Andy, you're the one I want to talk to. I understand you aren't very happy about the way the eminent domain case is being pursued against the marina, the diner and the bait shack."

"Who said that?! I don't have anything to say about it."

I tried to reassure him. "Look, I'm not going to tell anyone that I spoke with you, but you know what they're doing is wrong. Those people don't deserve to lose their livelihoods so that the developers can get richer, and I think you could be the key to stopping it."

"Listen, Mister Harper, I'd help you if I could, but I'd at least lose my job, and there are some powerful people involved in this thing. I can't risk it."

I hated to do it, but I had to learn what he knew. "Andy, I want to protect you, but I can't if you won't help me. The only other way to get what I need from you would be to ask your boss about it."

I heard a sharp intake of breath on the phone as I delivered the threat.

"Please. Don't do that." After a long pause, he said, "I don't feel safe talking over the phone. Can you meet me in an hour at the playground next to the elementary school? Nobody will be there at night."

"Thanks, Andy. You're doing the right thing. I'll be there."

I hoped he would show up.

Chapter Ten

When I drove up to the parking lot of the school, I could see the playground on the right, but saw no one there. Mine was the only car in the parking lot, and I wondered if Mays was going to show. I got out and walked over to the swing set, sitting in one of the vinyl slings that were a change from the wooden boards in the swings of my childhood. As my eyes got accustomed to the dim light, I saw movement by the climbing house at the edge of the playground. The two-story jungle gym had a slide and bridges on both sides, and as I walked over to it, I saw a figure sitting on a bench attached to the back. I spoke first.

"Hi, I'm Will. Thanks for meeting me."

"It's not like you left me a lot of choice."

"Andy, I wouldn't have pushed if I didn't have to. The people in those businesses are going to lose everything if the eminent domain case isn't stopped. I have the feeling you could be the key to that."

He sighed, and said, "What do you want to know?"

"I got the impression that you didn't see any need to get rid of the three buildings that they want for the park."

"Yeah, when we were doing the planning, I was assuming they would stay. Honestly, the design I recommended would have the park located behind the marina, and stairs going down either side of it. It made sense to me to make it the center of things because of the access it gives to boaters coming to the shops and restaurants. I was pretty shocked when my boss told me they wanted to tear it down."

"Your boss, Curt Stoneham?" I wanted to keep my facts straight.

"Yeah, that's him. He said that the developer wanted the old buildings and the marina torn down, and that the city would put in a park and a staircase to the riverfront on the site. I tried to convince him that it would save a lot of money to keep the buildings, and that they actually contribute to the atmosphere, but he wasn't even listening. He told me to shut up, and that if I wanted to keep my job, I'd make the changes on the drawings we submitted and keep my mouth shut about it."

He shook his head, looked bitter, and said, "When I studied city planning in college, it was all about making urban environments a better place to live. There hadn't been much of an opportunity to do that in a small town like Dolphin River, and when the new development came along, I was excited about it. Now I feel like a shill for the property developers, and I'm trying not to lose my job. This really sucks."

"I don't blame you for being unhappy about it, but just think how much worse it is for the owners of those three businesses. They are going to lose their jobs and their investment at the same time. It's totally unfair, and that's why I'm trying to stop it." I paused, and said, "Have you heard anything in the city planner's office to explain why Stoneham would ignore his own staff and do what Dolphin River Partners wants? I mean, this is a heck of a gift from the city to the developers, to build them a park and staircase to the river, and it sounds like the city might get stuck building boat slips as well. The question is why?"

Mays looked around nervously, checking to be sure no one could see our clandestine meeting. "Look, Mr. Harper, I want to help, but someone could go to jail over this. I've been told that if I rock the boat, they'll pin it on me."

"How would they do that?" I asked him.

"There's a guy, a rough looking dude named Bo Wolf, has tattoos all over his arms. He's been in and out of Curt's office a lot, so I think he works for him."

I said "I've run into him before."

"Anyway, I'd been talking to some of my co-workers about how unhappy I was about the developer getting this big gift from the city, and it must have gotten back to my boss. One night this Wolf guy showed up at my apartment, basically pushed his way inside. He threatened me. Showed me copies of cancelled checks from the developer made out to me, and said if I didn't keep quiet, that he would make it look like I'd been bribed. He also told me there were other ways I could get hurt. I got the message clear enough."

"Andy, I know there's a risk here, but letting them get away with a crime makes you guilty too. I'll do my best to keep you out of it, but I have to know why the city wants to do this giveaway."

He looked resigned, and said, "When this plan was first proposed, Dick Richmond from Dolphin River Partners was in and out of the planning office and the mayor's office so much, you'd think he worked there. It was an open secret that all the top brass in the city were being wined and dined, taken on junkets on the corporate jet, you name it. On one trip they flew four of them to San Antonio to look at their city's River Walk, which has turned into a big attraction. Some of the staff had to do a little covering up to make it look like they paid their own way, but it was fancy hotels, booze and hookers the whole way. It wasn't strictly what you'd call a business trip."

"Do you have any proof of this?"

"For my own protection I made copies of everything that came through the planning office about it, and I've got them in a safe at my house. Dawn, the mayor's assistant, was pretty unhappy about the wild partying she heard about, and I'll bet she's kept track of what he's doing. She and I talked a little before I got shut down by the threats, and I got the impression she was keeping copies of receipts for protection too. She's likely too scared to talk to you, though."

"Have you got any proof of actual payoffs to government officials, Andy?"

"No, but I'll tell you who probably does. Do you know who Mardy Jackson is?"

"Yes, I tried to interview him, and he threw me out."

"He's tight with the mayor, and Jackson has made a ton of money buying up property before the development was announced publicly. I guarantee you that he knows the money trail. Not that he'd ever help you."

"Good grief, is there anyone connected to city hall who isn't getting rich off of this?"

He looked miserable, and said, "Yeah, me. I never even saw the money from those checks they supposedly bribed me with. Wolf said they were in an offshore account in my name, but I don't know anything about it."

I gripped his arm, and said, "Andy, you're doing the right thing. For now, keep your head down and don't attract any attention. I think we have a fighting chance to stop the eminent domain case. Hold tight to your evidence, and don't tell anyone you've got it."

He looked at me with a glimmer of hope. "Right now, I'd settle for getting out of this with my career intact. I can't even quit and move away with this hanging over me. I'd never get another job without my boss's recommendation."

I smiled, and said, "With any luck, it will be Curt Stoneham who ends up without a job."

That was a promise I badly wanted to keep.

§

The next morning I called Walter to let him know that the Bait Shack and Diner owners were on board with joining Sandy's fight, and to fill him in on what I'd gotten from Andy Mays. He agreed to try and keep Mays out of it, and promised to send a letter right away to all of the city officials involved, challenging the legal basis for both the property condemnation and secondarily, for the values they were placing on the properties. It would be like kicking an anthill, and the fire ants we have in the south can be a nasty bunch when they are riled up. I didn't expect them to fight fair, and they didn't disappoint me. Within days of our attorney letter being sent, I got a threatening phone call from the city manager, Bill Bixler.

"Harper, I know you are behind this letter from the hot shot Atlanta attorney, aren't you?"

"Walter doesn't like to see honest businessmen get screwed, and that sure seems like what's been happening here."

I could feel his anger through the phone lines. "Look, Harper, a lot of people have invested in this project, and you can bet your ass no crappy reporter and his two-bit lawyer are going to stop it. You're letting yourself in for a world of hurt if you try."

"Why, Mr. Bixler, are you threatening me?"

"It's not a threat. If you don't back off, those people's businesses might find out they have a lot of code violations that will shut them down. Then they'll be worth even less than the generous offer we've made them."

"Bixler, using the power of the city government to persecute businesses that you're trying to get to move could well be considered an illegal conspiracy. You might want to think twice before you go that route."

"Well, you can consider yourself warned." I heard a loud click as he slammed down the phone.

This could be a problem, or it could be an opportunity, I thought.

Looking at my phone, I toggled to the nifty little app I'd downloaded last week that recorded incoming calls when you hit the 4 key. It had worked perfectly.

Chapter Eleven

The afternoon weather was sunny and mild for Florida, so I decided to take my little Boston Whaler tender over to the Dolphin River Marina and pay Sandy a visit. It would take a half hour in the boat versus ten minutes by car, but the scenery was worth the extra time. I puttered slowly out of my SailFin Point slip, past the rows of trawlers, passage-making sailboats and sport fisherman, then through the mooring field of weekender's day sailers before finally reaching the channel and getting up to speed.

Turning up the Manatee River, I kept my sixteen foot runabout out of the main channel, avoiding the wakes of the bigger boats heading out to Tampa Bay. The Whaler was a very seaworthy boat, but its low freeboard could make for a wet ride if you started bouncing over the wakes of larger vessels, and I didn't want to greet Sandy looking like a drowned rat. We hadn't spent a lot of time together since the eminent domain case had dropped a bomb into her life, and I wanted to rekindle our romance a bit.

When I turned off the Manatee into the smaller Dolphin River channel, I slowed to enjoy the view. Cypress knees, trees dripping with Spanish moss, and wild palms dotted the bank. Birds filled the trees, and it was easy to imagine what this landscape had looked like to the settlers a century ago, before developers began filling the bays to build more land for condos.

This part of Florida's West Coast isn't as overbuilt as areas like Orlando, Miami and Fort Lauderdale, but the growth shows no sign of stopping. There is just too much money to be made by bulldozing the trees in favor of shiny new buildings and local governments are too enamored of the larger tax base to stop it.

And they call it progress.

Dolphin River had been something of a sleepy little town, dwarfed by Bradenton next door, and far enough from the bay to escape the attention of big developers until now. It looked like that was coming to an end. As I glided the Whaler past old fishing shacks crumbling on the banks, I could see the construction trailers being set in place on the site of the new River Walk complex, just a couple of blocks from the Dolphin River Marina.

I was surprised that the building project looked like it would begin before the eminent domain case was resolved, but I suppose they planned on building it whether there was a park there or not. Maybe they didn't consider the possibility that they could lose the case, but Walter and I would do our best to stop them.

Slowing as I entered the No Wake zone of the marina, I pulled my boat into an empty spot near the gas docks and tied it to the cleats bolted into the wooden decking. Things looked slow, with more empty slips than I had remembered from my last visit. That didn't bode well for Sandy's finances.

I made my way up the docks to the marina office and opened the wooden door with the life ring bolted to the front for decoration. A window air conditioner was struggling against the humidity, unable to handle even a mild Florida day. Sandy was at her desk behind the counter, and looked up with a smile as she saw me.

"Will, this is a surprise." She stood and walked around the counter, pulling me into a tight hug. "What brings you here today?"

"Oh, it looked like a nice day for a boat ride, so I came over in the Whaler." I kissed her on the tip of her nose, and said, "And what brings me here is to see you." I pulled her into a real kiss, and we lingered in the moment, the only sound coming from the rattling air conditioner.

She leaned on my shoulder, and said, "I'm glad you're here. This was starting to be a crummy day."

"Want to tell me about it?"

She sighed, took my hand and led me out to the side porch, its lazy ceiling fan doing a better job of cooling than the old unit in the office. "Did you notice how many empty slips I have?"

"Yes, it was hard to miss. What's that about?"

"A lot of my most loyal tenants are leaving. I tried to tell them I was fighting the city, but when the construction trailers started moving in, many of them said they didn't want to deal with the noise and dust. I really can't blame them, but it's making it hard to hold on. I was having a tough time paying the bills already, and now... I don't know how long I can do this."

She looked so sad and lost, I badly wanted to give her good news, but I didn't want to give her false hopes. "I talked to Walter this morning, and he feels like he's making progress. He's called a few reporters he knows down this way, and they are interested in a story about what the development is doing to the town and to the businesses they want to move out."

She looked at me with hope in her eyes. "Will, do you *reely* think it will work?" Her French accent got thicker when she was upset.

"It's going to put pressure on the city, that's for sure. The city manager called me this morning, and he was pretty threatening. I got him on tape saying he'd use the building codes people to shut all of you down if you didn't go quietly."

She looked horrified. "Can they do that?"

I grinned at her, and said, "I'm sending the recording to Walter, and the first time they try it, he'll make it public. We couldn't use it in court, but it would sure be embarrassing for the city. Listen, it's no fun being threatened, but it tells you they are worried. You just have to hang in there until they crack."

"But what if they don't? I'll lose everything, and won't even have a job." I saw her struggling, and she finally looked up at me. "Do you think we could at least get the city to pay a fair price? I don't want to leave, but if I could pay the mortgage and have enough to pay back my parents for the money they loaned me, then I could live with myself. They can't lose their money too because of me."

"Sandy, don't give up yet. We've always known stopping the eminent domain was a long shot, but Walter seems to feel pretty confident that he can get the city to raise the price they have to pay if it goes forward. The bad publicity from screwing popular local businesses ought to make them more willing to negotiate. If they think they've got you on the ropes, they may hang tough. You can't let them know you're running out of money to keep fighting."

"But what do I do when I can't pay the power bill, the water bill, the mortgage?"

I struggled to answer her. I didn't want to tell her about the source we'd found in the city planner's office, at least partly because I'd promised him I'd try to keep his name out of it. It made me feel like we still had a real chance. I'd have to convince her to let me help. I took both her hands in mine, looked in her eyes, and said, "Sandy. I need you to trust me."

"You know I do, Will."

"Here's what I want to do. I'll loan you the money to keep the marina going, and you can pay me back when the city settles."

"NO! No, no, no, I cannot let you do *thees*! I won't take your money."

"It's not a gift, it's a loan. You know I can afford it, and I don't want to see you lose everything because they wait you out. The diner and the bait shack are solvent enough to stay open, and it's important you do the same. Consider it an investment."

"But what if the city never raises its price? Not only would my parents lose their money, but you would too. I can't do that to you."

"I'm in this fight too. Let me help you."

She put her head in her hands, and I understood why she felt so bad. Having no choice is tough for anyone, but it was especially galling for Sandy. A sailor, a free spirit, an entrepreneur with a dream, she hated to think that her life was in the hands of a greedy developer and his cronies in city government.

Finally, she looked up, determination on her face. "Will, if you do this, you must promise me that you will let me repay you with interest, right after the bank and my parents."

I breathed a sigh of relief. "You've got a deal."

With that out of the way, it was time for more serious business. "Can I interest you in a romantic dinner on my boat? I was thinking lobsters and wine. The deal includes pickup service and overnight accommodations."

Her beaming smile gave me her answer. "I'd love to."

I knew this trip would be worth it.

§

For just that night, we agreed to leave the legal and financial troubles of the marina out of the evening's discussion. No point in wasting good seafood and better wine by creating churning stomachs. After the meal was consumed, the dishes washed and we'd moved to the upper deck under the stars, I lay on an oversized chaise with Sandy curled up next to me, my arm wrapped around her shoulders.

"I wish it could always be like this," she said.

"Like what?"

"Oh, you know, wine, dinner, stars. None of the things we're not talking about tonight. Just simple enjoyment."

"If it was like this every night, we'd probably get bored."

"You know what I mean. I get tired of fighting to stay afloat."

"Not to get philosophical on you, but part of what makes me appreciate every day is not knowing how many you have left. Anyone can get hit by a bus, struck by lightning, hit by a meteorite." She looked at me skeptically, and I said "OK, maybe the last one was a stretch. The point is, we have to make the most of every day. It's why I quit my newspaper job when Dotty left me that money. Life is too short to spend it doing something you don't want to be doing, or working for people you don't respect. Every day is a celebration of the time we have."

"Oh, Will, I want this to last." She leaned up towards me for a kiss, then took my hand, pulled me up off the chaise, and led me down below to my cabin. As we stood beside the bed she kissed me passionately, and my hands explored her body in the heat of the moment. "Let's celebrate life tonight."

And so we did.

Chapter Twelve

Pressure is a funny thing. It can start gradually, and you don't even notice it. Then it comes at you from different directions, like an itch you can't reach to scratch, until you feel surrounded. And the pressure was definitely building on the people behind the land grab for Sandy's Marina.

First, there were the sympathetic news stories, telling of a slow way of life that would leave the city of Dolphin River when the marina, diner and the bait shack were pushed out. No more leisurely mornings on the river for the fishermen, with an early breakfast at the diner, fuel at the marina and bait from Bob's Bait Shack for their day of fishing.

The shiny new River Walk development would be a draw for the tourists, but there wouldn't be a place for the fishermen. The Bradenton paper did a poignant editorial bemoaning the loss of yet another piece of old Florida, and made a point of saying that the city's park and staircase was a million dollar gift to the developer.

There was no general call to stop the project, but the tone was shifting from unbridled support to a mixed message. Do we really need modern developments at the cost of losing the character of the few remaining sleepy rivers of Florida? I was surprised to see the usual civic boosters at the paper raise the question, and I knew the pressure was building.

When the local TV station's story on the city's move to force out the existing businesses was picked up by the national network, Dolphin River finally decided to respond to the criticism. Mayor Ferguson staged a press conference in city hall, with the architectural model of the development front and center. This time, the park and staircase were shown on the plans, and it did make an impressive display for the cameras.

I'd been tipped off by my newspaper contacts about the press conference, and noticed with satisfaction the sour look on the mayor's face when he spotted me in the crowd. He'd been answering questions from the press, painting a picture of only good things coming from the project. I raised my hand with a question and he did his best to ignore me, but I spoke up anyway.

"Mr. Mayor, what about the three businesses that are being forced out in the eminent domain case? This is certainly not a benefit to them."

There was a pause as the press awaited his response, and I could see sweat form on his brow under the hot TV lights. "The owners of the businesses are being well compensated for their loss. There's always a few people who get displaced in as big a project as this one. It's the price of progress."

"Actually, Mayor Ferguson, the amounts they've been offered are criminally low, and won't cover their debts on the properties, much less provide them with enough money to relocate. Not that you can relocate a marina, anyway."

"MISTER Harper, that is only your opinion. The offer is very fair."

It was the perfect time to spring my surprise. "Mr. Mayor, the attorney representing the three businesses has notified me this morning that he's filed suit to stop the eminent domain claim. Those businesses do not need to be moved for the project to be built, they can be adapted into it."

He looked stunned as I pulled an envelope from my pocket, stepped to the front and passed it to him. "That's the notice to the city of the lawsuit."

There was an uproar in the room as reporters and photographers gathered around me to get the story on the lawsuit. I had copies of the filing, and passed them out as I answered questions. A TV reporter stuck a microphone in front of me, and said, "And what is your connection to this case?"

"My name is Will Harper, and in the course of writing a story for *Florida Waterways* magazine about the River Walk development, I came to realize that moving those businesses was neither necessary to the project nor fair to the owners. I don't know what prompted the city to offer such a generous gift to Dolphin River Partners at the taxpayers' expense, but I'd love to hear what Mayor Ferguson has to say about it."

The cameras all swung back to the front, where 'Blackie'

Ferguson stood like a deer in the headlights. There was an uncomfortable pause, with the crowd awaiting his answer. He wiped his brow with a handkerchief, stuffed it in his pocket, and began speaking slowly.

"The city has worked with Dolphin River Partners to make this beautiful new complex one that will help our city bring in new residents, tourists and tax dollars. It seemed appropriate for the city to provide new road access, utilities and landscaping, and the park and staircase is part of that infrastructure. It is not a 'gift', as Mr. Harper says, it's an investment in this city's future."

The mayor was deluged with questions from the reporters as he finished his statement, and he declared, "This press conference is over," and fled the room. It obviously wasn't the impression he'd hoped to make. Taping ads for his car lot were a lot less stressful way to be on TV.

The reporters' attention swung back to me by default, and I answered their questions the best that I could. Our attorney, Walter Lord, had cautioned me not to say too much, to let the lawsuit dominate the headlines, but one question made me lose my restraint.

"Mr. Harper, do you believe that there are illegal payoffs behind the city's eminent domain effort against the marina and the other two businesses?" The TV reporter stood with her microphone thrust out at me, a look on her face that said she smelled a bigger story.

I tried to answer carefully. "I have no personal knowledge of any bribery of officials." Then I stuck my foot in it. "You might ask Mardy Jackson. He bought quite a lot of property near the River Walk site months before the project was announced."

A flurry of questions followed, and I fled the room as the mayor had done earlier. I'd stirred up a hornets' nest now, and they have a mean sting.

§

Before I even got back to my boat, the WanderLust, my cell phone was piling up voicemails. Most of it was reporters and I ignored those, but when I saw Walter's name pop up on the screen, I decided I'd better take that call.

"Hi Walter, did you catch the press conference?"

"Yes, I sure did. The local station down there was live streaming it, and I watched the whole thing." He paused and said, "It was going pretty well until you poked the snake."

"Sorry, Walter, I know you said to avoid making any accusations, and I didn't. Well, not exactly."

"Will, you know good and well that you made the suggestion that Mardy Jackson was a crook. Of course, he *is*, but you can't come out and say that."

"I know, I know. All I wanted was for the rest of the press to take notice and do a little investigating. There's no way he was smart enough to buy up all those shacky old houses unless he knew that the development would turn it into prime land. Somebody tipped him about the project, and I'd be willing to bet money changed hands for the information."

"You've certainly put him in the spotlight, and I guess that can't hurt too much. Try to remember though that our focus is on fighting the city over the eminent domain, not in rooting out everyone who's making money on the project."

"OK, I've got the message. How long do you think it will take the city to respond to the lawsuit?"

"They'll probably have their attorney draft an answer pretty quickly, and I warn you, judges tend to side with the local governments on this kind of thing. I still think the best bet is to shame them into a better settlement, but we have to at least look like we're trying to stop them from kicking out those businesses."

"What's the next step then, Walter?"

"If the judge shoots down our challenge, then I'm going to hit them with a settlement offer. I've talked to all of the owners, and we're going to ask for a million three."

"Wow. As in one million three hundred thousand dollars?"

"That's right. It breaks down to $700,000 for the marina, $350,000 for the diner and $250,000 for the bait shack. It would be enough for the three of them to pay off all of their debts and get a good start on new businesses."

"That won't be enough to fix Sandy's problem," I said. "Starting a new marina from scratch would cost well over a million dollars."

He sighed and said "I know, Will. The truth of the matter is that we don't expect the city to agree to that amount anyway. The three owners have privately agreed that the bottom line is $1,000,000 flat. Below that, they are all going to be pretty screwed."

This wasn't sounding good. "How much of that would go to Sandy for the marina?"

"She'd get $600,000. I know it's not great, but at least she'd be able to pay off all of her debts and have something to start somewhere else with. It would't be a marina, but there are other boat-based businesses she could go into."

"Geez, Walter, this won't exactly be a windfall for them, after all they've been put through by the city."

"I know that, Will, but there's no point in trying to win the lottery here. Eminent domain cases are based on fair market value for properties, and even with the new development, it's not as though they would have been instant millionaires. Every one of those properties needs substantial remodeling, and the judge will factor that in. The settlement I'm proposing is likely better than what we'd get in court. We just have to keep the pressure on the city, so that they realize it's in their best interest to offer a fair price."

"Walter, I know you're doing your best for them, I don't mean to sound like I'm complaining. It all just seems so unfair."

"Nobody ever said life was fair, Will. We have to fight to make it as fair as we can."

I couldn't argue with that.

§

It felt like the pressure had shifted from the city to us. The lawyers for the River Walk development had put out a statement blasting, "the reckless accusations being made against the city's support of this project," and Mardy Jackson had issued an angry denial that he'd done anything wrong. The city responded quickly to the lawsuit on the eminent domain case, and it was soon dismissed by a friendly judge.

Things were beginning to seem desperate. Sandy was depressed, feeling that her livelihood was slipping away, and I couldn't do much to ease her fears. We spent some time together, but they were all tinged with sadness. I was afraid that when the marina was gone, she would be too. The only option was to fight back with any tool left in the arsenal, and that meant calling Andy Mays.

I'd tried to leave him out of it, but he might be the last chance to stop this thing. It could cost him his job, but this was bigger than just him.

I waited until ten p.m. that night, trying to make sure he would be home and alone. Then I made the call.

"Andy? This is Will Harper."

I was greeted with silence.

"Hello?"

"I asked you not to call me again."

"Sorry, but you're my last hope. I need those documents you have that show the developers used money to influence the city government to build the park."

I heard a sharp intake of breath. "I can't do that."

"Listen, I know your job is on the line, but this is wrong, and you know it."

"It's not just my job anymore, Mr. Harper. That Wolf character has been following me around, and he's threatened me."

"Do you have anything you could go to the police with?"

"No, it's subtle. I'll find him leaning on my car, and then later find the tires slashed. I saw him walking past the neighbor's house, and then their cat turned up dead on my front porch. I admit it, I'm scared."

"Andy, believe me, I understand. But you've got to do the

right thing here. The only way to be safe is to expose them. They won't stop until you do."

After a long silence, he said, "Let me think about it."

"Just don't wait too long. Do the right thing, and protect yourself at the same time."

It was good advice. I wish he'd taken it.

Chapter Thirteen

Mardy Jackson was enraged. "I swear, I'm going to kill that damn reporter! He and that bitch that own the marina are behind all of these rumors flying around that I paid off the city for advance notice on the River Walk project."

Bo Wolf leaned on Jackson's desk as Mardy paced the room, uttering curses. Wolf was unruffled.

"That's because you did."

Jackson shot an angry look at his enforcer. "I'd better not ever hear you say that out loud again. You're as guilty as I am. You delivered the payoffs to Stoneham, and you're the one who strong-armed the homeowners who didn't want to sell. And, I might add, you were well paid for it."

Wolf gave a cold look to the angry developer. "You might want to watch what you say to me."

Jackson was angry, but not stupid. He put on the affable

face he showed to the customers. "Bo, hey, we're all friends here. I'm just trying to make sure we've covered our butts, that's all."

"Don't worry. I'll take care of it."

His tone did worry Jackson, though. "Don't do anything to make it worse, OK? Maybe just put a little scare into them, make them realize this fight's not worth the cost."

Wolf grinned, but the smile didn't reach his eyes. "I'll get their attention."

Mardy Jackson sat down at his desk, calmer now with the promise of action. "Thanks Bo, I knew I could count on you."

He only hoped his enforcer wouldn't go too far.

§

It had been a couple of days since I'd called Andy Mays hoping for a way to bust the city's case wide open, but so far, not a word. Sandy had been feeling low, and I invited her over to my boat for the evening for some comfort food; pasta, bread and wine. It was a hard dish for me to mess up, and as spacious as my boat is compared to most liveaboards, the galley is still a little tight for a gourmet meal, so easy was good. This visit wasn't really about food, though.

When Sandy arrived, she seemed down, but after a hearty dinner of angel hair pasta with meatballs, toasted garlic bread and substantial amounts of wine, her mood lightened considerably. My cash infusion into her marina had stopped the bleeding, and her bills were all current. At least for now, the pressure on her had dropped a bit, and she felt better about things. We sat on the upper deck of my boat under the stars, sipping our wine while lounging on the wide helm station seat. She leaned against the side with her legs across mine; I ran my hands up and down her smooth legs, enjoying the moment. Being a male, I hoped love making was in the plan for the evening, but alas, it was not to be.

"Will, I can't tell you how much I needed this. Thank you for taking me away from my problems for tonight."

"Always my pleasure, Sandy. Can you stay the night?"

"I wish I could. The company repairing the wiring on Dock Six is coming at seven a.m., and I can't afford to oversleep and not be there to meet them." She took my hand and said, "Sorry to disappoint you."

"Hey, I'm glad you came over. I can't help it if I hate for you to leave." I gave her a long kiss, our tongues dancing, and she finally pulled away, saying, "You're making this hard for me."

I couldn't resist. "I thought that was my line."

She giggled and said, "Men! I swear."

I put my arms around her. "I can't help it if you make me want you."

She kissed me again, pulled away and sat up. "Hold that thought, Will."

Soon, she was walking down the dock, heading back to her sailboat at the Dolphin River Marina, leaving me with empty plates, an empty wine bottle and an empty bed. Not the ending I'd hoped for.

I started doing dishes, and when my cell phone rang fifteen minutes later, I thought maybe she'd reconsidered.

When I answered, I could tell by her voice it was nothing good.

"Will, come quickly! Don't tell anyone what you're doing, just come now."

"Sandy, what's wrong?"

"I don't want to talk about it on the phone, just come now!"

Suddenly wide awake and wary, I raced down the dock to my Z4 and made it to the marina in minutes. I needed to stay calm, and walked to her slip trying to look casual about it. She'd sounded panicked on the phone, but her request to tell no one made me approach her boat cautiously. I walked around the sides of the slip to do a little reconnaissance, but the curtains to the Au Revoir's cabin were closed, only a small light showing through the edges of the heavy fabric.

There were no signs of anyone on deck, and I stepped lightly on board, moved to the cabin door, and slowly turned the knob. When I opened the door, she was there. Sandy pulled me in, closed it behind me, and pointed to the floor next to the settee. Andy Mays lay on the small rug, a pool of blood next to his head and a large wrench beside him. He stared at the ceiling with unseeing eyes.

The shit had hit the fan.

§

I took her in my arms, and said, "What happened?"

She sobbed into my shoulder. "I don't know! He was like that when I got here."

I held her for a moment, then directed her to a nearby chair. "Sit here while I check this out." There was no question that he was dead, but I wondered for how long. I put the back of my hand against his arm, and could feel that the warmth hadn't yet left his body. The blood was barely starting to congeal. She had just missed walking in on the murderer. "Sandy, do you recognize the wrench?"

"Yes. It's the one that I change the fuel filters with. I keep it in the engine compartment, I don't know how it got up here."

I had a pretty good idea. I'd be willing to bet that the only prints on that wrench would be hers.

"Will, who is this man? And why would someone kill him on my sailboat?"

I knelt in front of her. "His name is Andy Mays, and he works for the city. I'd been counting on him to help us stop the eminent domain case. Now I think someone is using him to stop us."

"But how? I didn't do anything, I was with you all night!"

"The killer cut it pretty close. He must have left right before you got here." This was all happening fast. I knew what would likely come next. An anonymous call to report a fight on her boat. The police were probably on the way right now. This frame was tight.

I knew what we needed to do, but I sure didn't like it.

"Start the boat, we've got to get this body out of here."

Her face was pasty, but she moved to the helm on the rear deck and cranked the engine. I hurried outside and cast off the lines. We backed out of the slip, moving slowly so as not to create a wake and disturb the other boats. Witnesses to a hurried departure wouldn't help things.

When the boat reached the channel, I directed her

downstream towards the Manatee River, then out into Tampa Bay. The water was too shallow to do anything except stay in the channel. It was a slow motion escape, made intensely nerve-wracking by the presence of the body below deck. I doubted anyone was chasing us yet, but there would likely be questions about our night-time excursion.

It was a long, tedious cruise through the edge of the giant bay, past Anna Maria Island, then finally out into the open ocean. My nerves were strung tight, knowing what came next. We'd broken the law now, but it was the only way out. Not that innocence would have helped with the neat frame that had been placed around Sandy.

The waves were fairly calm under the night sky, and the new moon gave us a darkness that was welcome. I could avoid it no longer. Returning to the cabin, I searched Mays' pockets, removing his wallet with its identifying photos, car keys and change. I walked to the stern and flung all of it into the water. The wrench went next, to the bottom of the ocean. No murder weapon to tie back to Sandy.

"I need you to help. Grab his feet." We carried him as far as the stern rail and set down his dead weight.

"Shouldn't we worry about fingerprints, DNA evidence, stuff like that?" Her face looked pinched in the dim light, and I knew what this was costing her.

"We're far enough out that it will be a while before his body turns up, if it ever does. The salt water will take care of the rest. Anyway, this boat is full of your DNA and mine. Hairs, flakes of skin, he probably has it all over him. That's why we had to come way out here."

She nodded that she understood, and I waited for her to gather herself for the task we had to do.

"Shouldn't we say something?" Sandy was raised Catholic, though I knew it had been a long time since she'd been to mass. But she was right.

"He didn't deserve this. He was just a scared little guy, trying to do his job. But the money people crushed him like they are trying to do to you. May God have mercy on his soul."

I reached for his shoulders and she took his feet, grunting as we lifted him over the rail to splash into the ocean. I'd thought about weighting the body with an anchor, but that would be evidence that could be tied to the boat. We watched as he floated away.

Sandy started the motor at my request, and we slowly pulled away from his watery grave. We still had to clean the boat of his blood, but it seemed like too big a risk to do the work with his body floating close by. After a couple of miles, she cut the engine, and we felt safe enough to turn on the cabin lights. She got out rolls of paper towels, and we blotted up as much blood as we could, tossing the debris over the rails. They would break down quickly in the water. I cautioned her to lean out before dropping them, to avoid anything dripping on the boat. I took the rug his head had laid on and cut it into small pieces with a carpet knife, throwing them in the water as I went. The knife went in after it. We worked on cleaning for nearly an hour, then double-checked behind ourselves with a very bright flashlight, until I was satisfied that we'd done the best job possible. It wouldn't stand up to a forensic examination, but with no evidence of a crime, that wasn't likely to happen.

She started the motor once more, and we made our way back to the bay and towards the marina. We talked little, but we got our story straight on why we'd taken her boat out at night. As we traveled, she went to take a shower. When she came out with a towel on her long hair, I traded places with her. I'd told her to be sure to scrub her fingernails, and I did the same. The water may have washed me clean, but I sure didn't feel that way.

All of my life, I'd been a rules follower. Not afraid to challenge authority when it was misguided, but not a law breaker either. I did things in a way that at least *I* felt were above board. Not this time. We'd moved and disposed of a body. We'd concealed evidence of a murder.

I didn't know if I'd ever feel clean again.

Chapter Fourteen

When we arrived back in Sandy's slip, the sun was coming up, and she had to head quickly for dock six and her appointment with the electrician. She felt like canceling, but agreed with me that trying to make things look as normal as possible was the best approach.

After she left, I made a pot of coffee and sat in the cockpit of her sailboat to watch the rest of the sunrise and try to calm my nerves after the awful night we'd just experienced. That's where I was when Enrique, Sandy's helper at the marina, called to me from the dock.

"Mr. Harper, is Sandy in there with you? The electrician was a little early, and he was looking for her."

"She's not here, Enrique. She already went to meet him on dock six."

He looked relieved. "OK, good. I was a little worried

when I came looking for her and saw the boat was gone."

I was afraid it would be noticed that her boat had been gone all night, but we'd already worked out our story. I looked a little sheepish and said, "Yeah, we had an argument last night, and decided to take the boat out so we didn't disturb anyone."

He looked worried. "Nothing serious, I hope."

"No, she's been under a lot of stress with this eminent domain case, and we just got cross with each other. It's all good now."

"Glad to hear that. It explains the mystery 911 call."

Oh shit. "What call is that?"

"Someone called from the pay phone at the marina laundry, said there was a big fight going on at this dock. The cops showed up, but it was all quiet. They asked a couple of the liveaboards, but no one else had heard anything. Just some damn busybody."

I looked concerned, and said, "Gosh, we weren't *that* loud. I can't imagine we disturbed anyone before we left."

"Ah, I wouldn't worry about it. The cops get prank calls all the time."

"I'll let Sandy know about it, just in case anyone has a complaint."

"Thanks, Mr. Harper. I'll be up at the office if Sandy needs me."

I'd been trying since I met him to get Enrique to call me Will, but he couldn't bring himself to do it. Old world habits die hard. I was relieved to see him go, and to find out that the police had blown off the noise report as a crank call. I'd been expecting an anonymous tip that there was a body on her boat, but I guess the killer had decided that was too obvious. It seemed a little bit of a gamble, since no one else heard anything and I wondered how he'd planned to get the cops to spot Sandy's boat and investigate it.

Curious, I climbed off the boat to the dock, and in the cloudy morning light took a close look around the hull. On the starboard side near the stern, I found my answer. A bloody smear dripped down the white finish of the sailboat. It was on the opposite side from where the boarding steps were, so we hadn't seen it, and it wasn't visible from aboard unless you leaned over the rail. The cops would have certainly found it if the boat had been in the slip when they arrived.

My nerves were jangling as I casually looked around, but no one else was on the dock or outside on their boats. I climbed aboard, located the cloth mop Sandy used for cleaning the cabin sole, and then leaned over the rail, dipped the mop in the water and quickly swabbed off the blood. I dunked the mop head in the water several times to rinse it, then squeezed it dry, removed the mop from the handle and placed it in a black trash bag for a quick disposal.

The murderer had set it up well, and the phone call was subtle enough to make it look like Sandy had been caught at the murder scene. Our late night excursion wasn't something they'd factored in, though, and someone was going to be very curious when nothing showed up in the news about a body being found.

I'd really like to know who that someone was.

The reality of Andy Mays' death weighed heavily on me.

He knew he was in danger, and my investigation into his boss's actions made them decide to shut him up. I never expected them to go as far as murdering a witness, but then, people had been killed for a whole lot less than the millions at stake in this project.

Staying on the boat was beginning to feel like a bad idea, so I locked the cabin, carried the trash bag to a rubbish bin on dock six, and walked down the dock to find Sandy. She was watching the electricians work, and I took her arm and walked her down the dock to a bench facing the river. She looked curiously at me, and I knew she wondered if there was more bad news.

"Sandy, the cops got an anonymous 911 call from the marina laundry to report a fight on your dock. When they showed up it was quiet, and no one else had heard anything, so they wrote it off as a prank call."

She leaned with a hand against her forehead, exhausted by the sleepless night. "That's a relief."

"There is one more thing, though. I wondered how the caller expected the cops to pick out your boat as the one the loud noise supposedly came from." She looked up at me, waiting for the other shoe to drop. "There was a bloody smear down the side of the boat, on the starboard side near the stern where you wouldn't notice it. I washed it off."

She put her face in her hands. "Oh God, this is a nightmare."

I couldn't argue with that. "We got lucky. Taking the boat

out like we did was a big risk, but I think you're in the clear for now."

"Will, I can't believe what we did. It's so *horrible*."

"I know, Sandy. Believe me, I feel awful about it. But the alternative was for you to be sitting in jail right now, accused of murder. And because you called me and I came to the boat, I might be in there too. At least this way, we're free to try and find the real killer."

She put her hand on mine, and said, "I'm so sorry I dragged you into this."

"It's OK, Sandy. You didn't know what to do."

I couldn't stop the thought in my head. *I wished she'd thought of something else.*

Now we were in it together.

§

Mardy Jackson paced his office like a caged tiger, raging as Bo Wolf sat looking relaxed in a padded chair.

"You KILLED him!? Didn't I say not to go too far? What the HELL were you thinking?!"

"Keep it down, Mardy, do you want your secretary to hear you?" He pulled out a long knife and began cleaning his nails with the point. The message was not lost on Jackson.

He sat behind his desk, and said, "What made you do that? Just explain it to me, please."

"The little rat was going to talk. I had a girl I know call Mays from a pay phone and tell him to meet me at this boat at the Dolphin River Marina. He thought he was meeting Will Harper."

"Great. Now there's one more person who knows about this."

"She doesn't know anything. All I had her do was make the call."

"Why did you want to meet him on a boat?"

Wolf leaned back and grinned. "It was Sandy St. Martin's boat. He'd brought all the papers he planned on using against his boss with him, thinking he was giving them to Harper. He tried to run out and I whacked him with a wrench. Guess I hit him a little too hard. Sorry about that."

Bo still held the knife, passing it back and forth from hand to hand, and Jackson knew he had to be careful. "Bo, did you leave fingerprints? Did anyone see you get on the boat?"

He looked irritated. "I'm not stupid. I wore gloves and a boiler suit, both of which are in the landfill by now."

"Did you take the papers he had on him?"

"Oh yes, I most certainly did. I have them stashed where they won't be found." He smirked, and said, "Never know when I might need a little insurance."

"That's Curt Stoneham's problem, not mine. It's his and the rest of those bozos at City Hall. I never leave a paper trail, not if it's something I don't want people to know about."

"Guess that's why you always pay me in cash. I'm thinking I might need a raise though, what with the risk I took last night."

Jackson took a deep breath. He knew he couldn't afford to piss off Bo Wolf. "We'll talk about it, OK? What's the fallout on May's disappearance? Did the cops arrest Sandy St. Martin?"

"I haven't heard anything yet. I've been checking the local news radio, but they may be keeping it quiet. Unless she's got a really good lawyer, she'll be in jail for a long time. It's her boat, and there's not that many places to hide a body on one."

"I hope you're right on that. We need to take the heat off the city on the eminent domain, and most of the heat is coming from her boyfriend. When she's locked up it will give him something else to worry about. If the city goes down on this project, I could lose a lot of money, and I don't need any of those cowards rolling over on me to get a lighter sentence."

Bo stood up, put the knife back in his pocket, and gave Jackson a hard stare. "If anyone ever tried that on me, the sentence wouldn't be lighter. It would be permanent."

The warning couldn't have been any clearer.

Chapter Fifteen

Where was the body? Bo Wolf paced the floor of his shabby trailer on the edge of town. It had been nearly a week since he'd killed Andy Mays, and there was no report of a body being found. That bitch that owned the marina had messed up his plan. It was the only thing he could figure out.

Somehow she'd managed to get the body out of there before the cops showed up. And what was the quickest way to do that? Of course. She'd taken the boat offshore and dumped the body. *Well, damn.* It was the only answer.

Bo had counted on her panicking when she found the body, but she must have stayed pretty cool to deal with it as she obviously had. He'd lied, of course, when he told Mardy Jackson he hadn't meant to hit Andy Mays that hard. That had always been the plan. Kill Mays, and lay the blame at the feet of Sandy St. Martin. Kill two birds with one stone, as it were.

Now he had a missing body, and apparently, nobody looking for it. When Mays didn't show up for work, police had gone and searched his house, but found nothing out of place. His car had been found at the marina, but that seemed a minor mystery to the cops. Everybody knew he was unhappy at his job. Maybe he just decided to disappear, the police concluded, and left his old beater of a car behind.

Damn, damn, damn.

Wolf had lots of money hidden in jars buried in the yard, and he struggled with his next step. Take the money and run? Or maybe stick it out for the bigger payoff at the end. Killing Mays had been a business decision, and he wouldn't lose a minute's sleep over it. His attempt at framing St. Martin would have given the cops an obvious suspect, their favorite kind. If the body turned up now, they'd be looking at anyone with a motive, and there were more than a few people who knew about the subtle threats he'd aimed at Andy Mays.

It was time to shake a little more cash from his benefactors, and be ready to leave town in a hurry. He might even indulge himself in a little payback as a farewell gift.

§

I didn't know it at the time, but I was worried about the same thing that Bo Wolf was. Would the body turn up? Sandy and I had gone far enough out into the ocean that there was a good chance it would be consumed by sharks or smaller fish before it had time to drift into the beach. We'd also avoided sport fishing areas, so it was unlikely that it would be spotted by another boat.

Waiting for something to happen and hoping that it wouldn't were a special kind of stress, and a week was a long time to deal with that stress with nothing else to distract me. I hadn't even been able to consider working on my writing, not with the constant stream of worry running through my brain.

Maybe it was time for some action to shake things up.

I got in my car, put the top down to brighten my morning and drove down to the county courthouse where the property records were stored. I'd see just how many properties Mardy Jackson had snatched up before the River Walk development was announced, and how far back those purchases started.

Finding a few of the former property owners wouldn't be a bad idea either. They'd likely been dismayed when the project became public, having already sold their now valuable land to the unscrupulous Jackson for much less than they could have gotten by waiting. Maybe a group of them might want to sue the bastard.

I felt better already.

After parking in the shade of an old oak tree dripping with Spanish moss, I made my way to the quiet records area. They had a pair of computers tied in to the Real Estate sales records, and while much of the information was available online, this was the most complete and up-to-date version.

Within an hour, I had much of what I needed, and it was no surprise. Mardy Jackson had purchased 37 houses and lots in the past five months, paying from as little as $9,000 up to $87,000 for one house on a large double lot. He'd spent a large amount of money in total, more than $850,000, but that land would soon be worth millions.

I'd had been thinking of Jackson as a minor player in what I believed was a conspiracy to let the River Walk project funnel cash to some of the members of the city government, but I might have to revise my thinking on that.

It was plenty of money to be worth killing someone for.

With a list in hand of the people who'd sold their land to Mardy Jackson, I used my iPhone to run down their addresses. Some of them had moved to other towns after selling their homes in Dolphin River, but quite a few of them lived in a trailer park on the edge of town. I started my car and drove in that direction.

The park was old, but not bad looking, with dated single-wides but mostly neatly kept yards. I parked my Z4 in front of a rundown trailer that seemed empty, planning to walk to the addresses I'd found in the park. Having a flashy car might make them more suspicious of my motives and that wouldn't help get them to talk to me.

The first door I knocked on went pretty much like I expected.

"Who is it!?" The voice was an older man's, and the TV was on pretty loud.

I yelled through the door, "My name is Will Harper, Mr. Williams, I'd like to talk to you about the property you sold to Mardy Jackson."

The TV went silent, and I heard feet shuffling to the door. It was yanked open, and an elderly man in need of a bath and a shave stood there in pajama pants and a ratty bathrobe.

"Who the hell are you? I've got nothing to say about that thieving bastard."

"My name is Will Harper, and I'm trying to find people who sold their homes and land to him shortly before the River Walk project was announced. If he had advance knowledge, the sales might be illegal."

"What's done is done. I've been screwed pretty much all my life, and this time is no different."

And with that, he shut the door in my face.

I got similar responses on the next three houses, ending with doors shut in my face. They'd all been cheated, but they didn't trust some stranger to make it any better. The next door I knocked on, I finally made some progress.

A chunky woman in a housedress answered the door. She had her hair fixed neatly, and smelled of baby powder, a much more pleasant odor than I had encountered thus far.

"Can I help you?"

"Yes, my name is Will Harper. I'm looking for a Mr. Gene Cramer?"

She looked doleful, and said, "He's here, but he had a stroke last month. He can't talk. I'm his wife, Myrna."

"Maybe you can help me then. I wanted to talk to your husband about the property he sold to Mardy Jackson three months ago."

She stepped quickly out onto the tiny porch, shut the door behind her and said, "Please, don't say that name where he can hear you. He hates that man."

"Can you tell me why?"

"My husband sold him the house we'd lived in for 24 years and moved us to this damn trailer park. Gene was convinced the money he got from Jackson was the most we'd ever get for that place, and ever since he lost his job at the Ford dealership, we've been struggling to get by. I have to admit, selling seemed like the right thing to do at the time. Gene had lost a couple of fingers in a wood shop accident and he couldn't work as a mechanic anymore."

"That does sound like a tough spot to be in, Mrs. Cramer. Why did that make your husband hate Jackson, though?" I thought I knew the answer, but wanted it in her words.

"Because almost before the ink was dry on the deed, they announced that $65 million dollar project three blocks from our house. I can't even imagine what that land is worth now. Gene went crazy. He was screaming that he'd kill Mardy Jackson and I was worried that he meant it. He raged for a week, then one day he just fell over." She looked down at her feet, and wiped her eyes before she looked back up at me.

"The stroke took his voice, and he's weak on the right side, too. It was bad enough that it should have killed him, but they got him to the hospital real quick, so the damage wasn't any worse. They keep telling me how lucky he is."

She looked so sad, I didn't know what to say. "I'm so sorry, Mrs. Cramer."

"You know what the worst thing is? If Gene hadn't of had that stroke, we could have been happy. This place isn't really so bad, and we had each other. He was always a good provider, right up until the accident. He was making me new cabinets for the kitchen, and sliced those fingers right off with a table saw."

There was really nothing to say to that.

"Now he sits there all day, can't speak, and I have to help him up to change his diapers. I blame Mardy Jackson for that stroke." She gave me a bitter smile, and said, "You know what else sucks? We rent this trailer from him. Every damn month, I write a check to Mardy Jackson."

§

It was late afternoon, and I was depressed and hungry. I'd made a lot of progress in locating disgruntled sellers, but hearing their stories wore on me. I drove over to Bradenton to a nice little seafood shack, had some fried clams and a beer, and tried to boost my flagging energy.

The more I learned about the River Walk project's impact on the town, the more I wished there was some way to stop it completely. That was pretty unlikely, though. The old saying "You can't stop progress" really means that you can't stop people with money from rolling over the people without it, all so they can grab a little more.

I'd always believed capitalism was a good thing, but this nest of thieves was enough to make a guy believe in socialism. The real problem, though, wasn't the form of government, it was the corruption that large amounts of money brought to it.

Money was the key here. Big money was behind this project, and a lot of people wanted their cut. Mardy Jackson had gotten his at the expense of poor homeowners, and the city was getting theirs at the expense of Sandy's marina, the bait shack and the diner.

Maybe the way to unravel this was to start costing them some of that money.

Chapter Sixteen

Walter Lord didn't have any good news when I called him. He'd heard nothing back from the city on his settlement offer in the eminent domain case, and that wasn't a good sign. I told him about my research into the land purchases Mardy Jackson made, and he thought it might be a good way to ratchet up the pressure on city hall.

"Will, if you can get a group of unhappy sellers to join as a party to a lawsuit, I can file one against Jackson claiming that he used insider information provided by the city to defraud the sellers. It might not get very far without any real evidence, but if a judge doesn't dismiss it outright, the publicity will be pretty rough on Jackson, the city, and Dolphin River Partners."

"Good. I want to keep the spotlight on them."

He chuckled, and added, "You do have a way of pissing people off, don't you, Will?"

He didn't know the half of it.

"Waiting for things to happen has been wearing on me, Walter. I feel like I have to do something."

I told him a few of the hard luck stories I'd heard from people who'd sold to Jackson and he agreed that the harsh light of publicity would make the developer look bad.

"Everybody pretty much accepts that the developers are the ones who make money in those deals, but when somebody like Mardy Jackson, who's not even involved in the River Walk deal, makes out like a bandit while screwing the landowners, it puts a stain on the whole project. That's not something that either the city or Dolphin River Partners can afford to let happen."

"But Walter, what can they do about it? They don't own those properties, Jackson does."

I could almost hear the wheels turning over the phone. "Well, they could pressure him to make additional payments to the sellers, or face zoning problems when he wants to build on any of that land." He thought a moment, and said, "I guess that seems pretty farfetched, since the city is screwing its own set of landowners with the eminent domain case."

"I'm pretty mystified, Will, that they haven't upped their offer for Sandy and the others. It's not that much money in the grand scheme of things, and if we generate enough bad publicity for the city, the pressure will continue to grow against them. It's like they think they can't lose."

"We've got to keep fighting, Walter. I'll talk to as many of the sellers as I can and see who's willing to sign on to the lawsuit."

"Don't make them any promises. This won't cost them anything, but the odds are long on them getting anything out of it."

I said, "Based on the ones I talked to so far, they are an angry bunch. They feel powerless, and the chance to hit back is going to feel pretty good. I'll keep you posted on my progress."

We said our goodbyes, and I felt the weight of the secret I was keeping from him. Not that I had much choice. Letting our attorney know that Sandy and I had disposed of a body seemed like a *very* bad idea.

§

It was late in the afternoon when I got back to the WanderLust, and I was beat. Searching property records had been dull work, but it was easier than dealing with the rage I felt from Mardy Jackson's victims. I opened a beer and sat on the upper deck, trying to clear my head. I turned when I heard my name called from the dock below.

"Yo, Will, permission to come aboard."

"Hey, Rick, get yourself a beer from the fridge and come on up."

"Don't mind if I do."

My stomach was in a knot as I waited for him to climb up and join me. It had been his tip that had led me to Andy Mays, and I felt responsible for May's death.

Captain Rick sat down across from me in one of the deck chairs, put his feet up on a chaise, and took a long drink of his Red Stripe. "How's it going, Will? You look like you haven't been sleeping."

"Fighting the city for the marina and the others is starting to wear on me, Rick. It's like pushing a big rock uphill. Every time you stop to rest it rolls back over you."

He grinned, and said, "Yep, that's what fighting against the government sounds like to me. Making any progress?"

"So far the city won't bend at all. I talked to Walter about it today, and he said it's like they think they can't lose." I paused, and said, "Makes me wonder what their ace in the hole is."

"Now see, that's where I think you're wrong, Will. The reason they believe they'll win is because they are *the government*. Taxpayers pay for their lawyers, and they can sue, countersue, appeal, harass the plaintiffs, anything they want, and it doesn't cost them a dime. It's not their money."

He took another sip of his beer, and said "It's a big game to them, playing with other people's money. You are playing with real money and they aren't."

"I never thought of it that way. Maybe you're right."

"Damn right I am. You're at least making them look bad, though, and the money folks behind that fancy project don't like bad publicity. Have you found anything you can use against them yet?"

"Most of what I've come up with so far looks bad for Mardy Jackson, not the city. I know he got tipped off about the development plans by someone, but the hard part is finding out who and then proving it."

He looked down at the deck, then glanced up and said, "Heard anything from Andy Mays?"

I couldn't stop my face from coloring, but tried to answer safely. "No, and I feel really bad about that. I thought he was going to help us, then he just disappeared."

"Yeah, I know. My friend Jim is kind of pissed that I gave Andy's name to you. His girlfriend's daughter is all bent out of shape since he's vanished, and she thinks something happened to him. Says he'd never have left without her."

Lying to Captain Rick felt awful, but there was no choice. "I'm sorry you're in the middle of that. I warned Andy that keeping the evidence he had locked up wasn't a safe approach, but he was afraid to come forward. I do hope he's all right, and just hiding out." The image of his body facedown in the water, floating away from Sandy's sailboat would always haunt me, and I choked up thinking about it.

Rick put his hand on my arm, and said, "Hey, Will, it's OK. It's not your fault that any of this happened, and Jim will get over being mad. Maybe Andy will turn up when all this blows over."

I didn't have an answer for that.

Rick stayed a while to talk fishing, since it was apparent to him that I'd talked about Sandy's problems as much as I could handle for one night. When he finally got up to leave, he looked at me and said, "Listen, Will, don't let all of this make you crazy. No matter what happens with the city and the River Walk, the sun will still come up tomorrow. I've seen a lot of changes in my years in Florida, a lot of them bad, a few of them good. Things have a way of working out."

"Thanks, Rick. I needed to hear that." I only wished it had worked out better for Andy Mays.

§

Sandy called me as the last of the sun was setting, and said, "This has been a good day for me. Take me to dinner."

"What made it such a good day?"

"Pick me up in 45 minutes, and I'll tell you all about it. Wear your gray jacket."

"OK, see you then." My gray jacket was a sport coat, a cashmere blend that was so soft I had to stop Sandy from rubbing a hole in the sleeve when I wore it. Looked like it would be a fancy evening. I hadn't been in much of a mood to go out, but I knew we would avoid talking about painful subjects in a restaurant. Maybe it would lift my spirits.

When I pulled up at the end of Sandy's dock, she was standing by the ramp, illuminated by the caged light on the pole over the sign that said "Dock Tenants Only". She looked beautiful in a black cocktail dress.

I walked over to her, and she said, "Hey sailor, give a girl a lift?"

Taking her in my arms, I gave her a long kiss. "Looking like that, I'm lucky no one beat me to it."

"*Oui*, you are a verrrry lucky man, Will. Perhaps you will become even luckier."

This dinner invitation was sounding like a better idea by the moment.

"And where would mademoiselle like to be taken?"

"I was thinking of the Beach Bistro over on Anna Maria

Island for dinner. As for where I shall be taken, that is a question for later, *mon ami*."

I love it when she's flirty.

Offering her my arm, I walked her to my car, helped her in, and slid behind the wheel. A beautiful woman, a sexy car and a moonlit night, what could be better.

The restaurant was darkened for the evening crowd and while we drank wine and awaited our dinner, Sandy told me about her day.

"Will, I rented two slips today! They are short term rentals, so the rates are higher, which actually helps me right now. The owners are friends who wanted slips next to each other, and that was harder to do at fancier marinas like SailFin Point. They will stay as long as they can, but made the leases short term because of 'That thing about which we do not speak.'"

I was relieved to hear that the eminent domain case would not be a topic tonight, and clinked my wine glass against hers. "I'll drink to that."

The food was wonderful. She had the house special, "Grouper Cooper," a pan-seared grouper, topped with a butter-poached lobster tail and aurora cream, and I had the six ounce prime rib, medium rare, with a lobster tail added on. It was a decadent meal, and when I ordered the crème brûlée for dessert, I wondered how I'd be able to finish it.

That turned out not to be a problem, as Sandy, who *never* eats dessert, ate most of it.

It was a perfect evening, and we took off our shoes and walked on the beach in front of the restaurant to work off the huge dinner.

She took my hand while we danced away from a wave as it moved further onto the beach, and squealed when the chilly water splashed her bare legs. We walked over to a wooden bench facing the water and sat, my arm around her neck as she leaned on my shoulder.

"Ah, Will, this has been a wonderful evening. Thank you."

"My pleasure. It's been nice to get away from... everything."

We sat for a long time watching the waves crash in the moonlight, then she said, "Take me home now. I want to be loved, and I want to be held." We walked to my car. "Put the top down. Let me feel the night."

The top had stayed up for the drive over, but she wasn't worried about her hair or makeup now. I drove through the streets back to the bridge to the mainland, and as we crossed the darkened span, she threw her head back and stared at the stars, her hand finding mine in the dark.

The smile on her face was worth it all.

Chapter Seventeen

Waking up with Sandy next to me in my bed made a great start to the day. Later I wished we'd stayed there all day.

After morning coffee and a Danish, she needed to be taken back to the marina. Sandy kept a few basic toiletries and some clothes on my boat, so she was spared a 'walk of shame' up my dock in last night's cocktail dress. When we drove up to the marina office, I saw Enrique out back, looking up at the telephone wires into the building.

"Good morning Enrique, is everything all right?"

"Hello Miss Sandy, Mr. Harper. This phone is not working." He stared up at the wire that should be hanging from the pole to the building. "Looks like it's been cut."

"*Merde*! I've been waiting for something like this. Is everything else OK on the property?"

He looked sorrowful, and said, "The skiff we use for

running around the marina sank at the slip sometime last night. It's still tied to the dock by two lines, but the motor is under water. I came up to the office to call you about it, and that's when I found out the phone was dead."

She sighed. "I'll call the dock repair company. They have a barge with a small lift on it, so we can get the motor out before the water ruins it."

Enrique went back into the office, and I took Sandy's hand. "Is there anything I can do?"

With a rueful smile, she said, "Thanks for last night. I needed the break, but I knew this wasn't going away. Just keep working to stop them, while there is still something left to salvage."

"Look at it this way, Sandy. Somebody must be getting nervous. They've got to hope that you'll get tired of fighting."

"I can't give up Will. This marina and my boat are all I have. Walking away isn't an option."

She was right about that. It wasn't for me, either.

§

The vandalism wasn't a surprise. I'd been expecting it all along, but had been more surprised that their tactics jumped straight from vague threats to murder. It made me wonder if the people behind it weren't all on the same page. I decided to keep working on the most promising angle, and that was to gather unhappy sellers for the lawsuit against Mardy Jackson. I spent the afternoon tracking down as many of them as I could, and none of them were happy about the deals they'd made with Jackson.

They had one big thing in common. They all felt cheated. After the initial stonewalling I'd gotten in the trailer park, word had spread about what I was doing, and doors began to open easier. People were more willing to talk, but the stories just got worse.

I knew when the worn, wrinkled woman with the white hair and the nut-brown skin answered the door that her sorrowful expression had a reason. She showed me into her tiny living room, the furniture old but neat, shelves covered with family photos. She pointed to one, of her and a saggy-faced man with a nasal cannula over his lips. "My husband, we'd been married 49 years. He had emphysema, but they call it COPD these days, I guess. He knew he didn't have all that much longer, and he wanted to leave me with something, so when that Mardy Jackson showed up at our door offering to buy the old place, he was so happy."

She fidgeted with her hands, and said, "No one had ever given us anything, you know? I told Melvin that the money wouldn't last that long, that we should just stay, but he wanted me to have money in the bank. It really wasn't even that much, not to give up our house after all those years in it. We moved in here, and Melvin was happy at first. Then they announced that River Walk project and he figured out that we'd been cheated. After that, well, he just quit caring about living." A tear ran down her cheek, and she said, "Then he died."

There didn't seem to be much else to say, though I offered my condolences. I got up to leave, and at the door, she grabbed my arm. "Mr. Harper, we worked hard all our lives, never asked help from nobody. I'm used to living without things, but I never thought I'd lose my Melvin to a broken heart. It killed him way before his lungs gave out. What that man did was wrong, and I want to see him pay for it. I'll sign on to your lawsuit."

That was at least two deaths that could be blamed on Mardy Jackson. I wondered if Andy May's death was the third.

§

When I walked out of her front door, I spotted Bo Wolf leaving the trailer next door. He moved away quickly, and I knew his presence wouldn't be a good thing. I went to the trailer, climbed the steps to the door, and started to knock. I stopped when I heard a low moan come through the thin aluminum wall.

"Hello? Is somebody hurt in there?"

"Go away, leave me alone, I've got nothing to say to you."

I wasn't giving up that easy. "Sir, it sounds like you may be injured. If you don't come to the door, I'll have to call 911." There was no answer, but I heard a loud groan as feet shuffled towards the door. It cracked open slightly, leaving the person behind it in shadow.

"There's nothing wrong with me, I just fell and hurt my back. Now leave me alone."

"Not until you open this door and let me see that you're all right."

The door creaked open a little farther, and a portly middle-aged man leaned around it. Past his bulk I could see a broken chair and a shattered lamp on the living room floor. He had pain showing on his face, and I wondered how Bo Wolf had hurt him.

"Did the man I just saw leaving do this to you?"

His eyes widened with fear, and he said, "I told you, I fell! Nobody did anything to me. Now leave me alone." He shut the door in my face, and I wondered how many more takers I'd get on the lawsuit when word of this attack spread. It was time to visit Mardy Jackson again.

§

The drive to Jackson's office didn't take long, and I walked into his office without invitation. He was on the phone, and when he looked up and saw me, he abruptly hung up.

"What do you want? I'm busy here."

"I want you to call off your attack dog, Jackson."

He tried looking indignant, but it wasn't working. "I have no idea what you're talking about."

"Sure you do. Bo Wolf has been skulking around your trailer park and beat up one of the victims of your scam. If this winds up in court, that could be intimidation of a witness," I said.

"You're flirting with slander there, Harper. Purchasing property from willing sellers isn't a crime, last time I checked."

"Maybe not, but I'll bet that using insider information obtained with bribes to defraud those sellers *is* a crime. You'd better put Bo Wolf back on a leash before he makes things worse for you."

I was pleased to see Mardy Jackson finally look nervous. "I have no control over anything he does, he's not my employee. I'm a legitimate businessman, not some crook. Get out of my office, right now."

"My pleasure, Jackson, the stink in here is starting to get to me." It was melodramatic, but hey, things felt that way. It seemed like half the town was involved in this thing.

§

Mardy Jackson picked up the phone as soon as Harper left his office and the front door closed. He called Curt Stoneham at the City Planners Office. "Curt, it's Mardy. Listen, Will Harper is running around interviewing everybody I bought property from that's anywhere near the River Walk project. Your guy Bo Wolf beat up one of them, and I'm worried about what else he may have done. You need to send him on a long trip."

"Mardy, he's not 'my guy', I just introduced you to him. If you hired him, that's on you. I've got enough to deal with here without worrying about your problems. The mayor has been all over me about why we agreed to build that park for River Walk. Never mind that he thought it was a great idea before the pushback started."

Now Jackson was worried. "Nothing's happening to slow down the project, is it?"

"No, but the mayor is getting tired of the bad publicity. He wants to get the eminent domain finished and those buildings gone so they won't be in the news any more."

"Maybe I should do the same thing, Curt. Bulldoze some of those houses I bought before anybody makes a big deal out of it."

"Don't count on getting demolition permits from the city right now, Mardy. We've got enough problems around River Walk and we don't want to stir up more trouble."

"Listen Stoneham, you were well paid for the information that led me to buy those properties. You'd better clear the way for me when I'm ready to start developing them."

A long silence followed. "Mardy, be careful what you say. You never know who's listening." He paused, and said, "I won't hang you out to dry. You have to be patient, that's all."

"Don't make me wait too long," Jackson said, then slammed down the phone.

He stared at the silent phone, and thought, *If I go down, I'll be sure to take a few of them with me.*

Chapter Eighteen

The news from our attorney was discouraging.

"Will, it looks like the city is going to win the eminent domain action. I've done everything I can think of, but the judge seems to believe that the park and staircase are a legitimate public benefit. I've tried to get our position across to him, that it's a big gift to the developer, but he doesn't see it that way. The trend the last few years has been for municipalities to grow their tax base by making sweetheart deals with developers, and the courts don't seem inclined to put a stop to it. I wish I had better news," he said.

It was pretty depressing. "So is that it, Walter? Sandy loses everything?"

"Now, Will, I didn't say that. We still have a good case that they are trying to undervalue the three properties."

"What happens next?"

"There will be a hearing on what the real value should be, and the judge will probably try to get the two sides to settle out of court. So far, the city won't budge. If we don't come to an agreement, the judge and a jury will hear testimony from both sides about what the actual value should be, and then make a decision. We have a pretty good argument that they aren't being fair, so I'm hoping we can push the price up substantially."

"Are we stuck with whatever the court decides?"

"Either side can appeal the decision, but the city will be fighting it on the taxpayer's dime. Appeals could take years, and as much as I want to help with this, I couldn't take on a bunch of appeals. I'm sorry, Will."

"You've got nothing to apologize for, Walter. I never expected you to do this for free. I was willing to pay your fee."

"I know, but I was glad to do it, I owed you one, remember? And you *are* going to get a substantial expense bill. I can't expect my staff to donate their time."

"It will be my pleasure to pay it." Once again, I silently thanked my aunt Dotty for the inheritance that made it possible. I only hoped it wouldn't end up being a wasted effort.

§

Mayor Blackie Ferguson was angry, and his secretary, Dawn DeLuca, was feeling it.

"Dawn! Get in here."

She rushed to his office door, and said, "What's wrong, Mr. Mayor?" She called him Blackie when things were calm, but had a feeling the more formal title might be a safer alternative at the moment.

"Get Curt Stoneham up here now! And put a call in to Dick Richmond at Dolphin River Partners. Tell him I need to meet with him today."

"Yes sir." She raced back to her desk and called Stoneham in his office at City Planning. "Curt, it's Dawn. Listen, Blackie is on the rampage, and wants to see you in his office right away." She smiled nervously at his answer, and said, "Yes, it was wonderful, but we'd better not talk about that now." She hung up the phone and sighed. Getting involved with a married man was stupid, and she knew it. He'd swept her off her feet with flowers and cards that had the rest of the office wondering about the identity of her "Secret Admirer". She'd gone out with him only when he promised to stop sending them.

She'd found him unexpectedly charming, and the expensive dinners and gifts he gave her didn't hurt. His wife traveled for work and was gone a lot, and the affair became hard to end. Now things were getting intense, as Curt told her that he was coming into a large sum of money, and that when he did, they should move to Costa Rica together and get married. She was worried about where that money would come from, and feared that it had to do with the River Walk.

Placing her second call, she got Dick Richmond on the phone. "Hello, Mr. Richmond? This is Dawn in the mayor's office. He asked me to call and see if you were available to meet this afternoon. Uh huh. Well, it did sound pretty urgent. Could you come over to City Hall at four? That's good, thanks you so much."

This was all starting to make her uneasy. When the River

Walk development had been announced there was a lot of smiles and backslapping in the mayor's office, but the atmosphere in the last couple of months had become tense. Curt and the mayor hadn't been expecting the pushback from the small businesses on the eminent domain, and now the lawsuit had attracted a lot of negative attention.

Then Andy Mays disappeared. He'd been the only person she could talk to about her concerns over the River Walk project, and now he was gone. Blackie and Curt seemed too friendly with the developer to make her believe that the public interest mattered much to them, but she didn't know what she could do about it. She thought, *I only hope that Andy is OK.*

Dawn kept copies of receipts from every trip, dinner expense and meeting concerning the project, but she was too afraid to tell anyone. Her affair with Curt Stoneham would likely be exposed if she did. In addition to the public humiliation, she'd be out of a job. Her best bet seemed to be to keep her head down and wait.

§

A few minutes later, Curt Stoneham strolled into her office. "Hey baby," he whispered.

Dawn's eyes got big, and she shook her head to warn him. "Yes, Mr. Stoneham, the mayor is expecting you. Go right in."

He licked his lips and leered at her. "Thank you, Miss Deluca." He leaned in and tried to kiss her, and she swiveled her chair away in alarm just as the mayor stuck his head out the door.

"Curt! Quit bothering my secretary and get your ass in here. We've got problems."

Stoneham entered the office, shut the door, and loud voices soon sounded behind it. Dawn knew it was a risk, but she opened the intercom circuit to the office and said "Sir, would either of you like coffee?"

"Not now, leave us alone." The mayor turned back to Stoneham. "Damn woman doesn't know when to stay out of my way sometimes."

Her nerves made her hand shake as she put the voice recorder next to the phone. The mayor had complained for weeks about the lights on his phone being out, and she was counting on it now. Protecting herself meant knowing what was happening, and this seemed like the only way.

"Curt, what the hell is going on with this project? I'm getting clobbered in the media over the eminent domain case, and now the Bradenton paper is running stories about Mardy Jackson buying up properties. Did you tip him off before River Walk was announced?"

"Blackie, you know I'd never do anything like that."

"Then how did he know to spend all that money on derelict properties? All of the land that development will be on was bought through shell companies just to avoid this kind of thing. It makes us all look bad, like we're giving favors to our friends, dammit."

Stoneham started to sweat. "Honestly sir, the only thing I can think of is that he saw the pattern of land purchases and figured it out. He watches the real estate transactions around here like a hawk."

The mayor snorted. "More like a damn vulture, I'd say."

He paced the office, and said, "Explain to me again how this park and staircase plan came about. I mean really, why are we spending this much money on a green space in the middle of their $65 million dollar project? Seems like they could afford to do it themselves."

"Mr. Mayor, you know we've been trying to get this kind of signature project built in Dolphin River for years. Manufacturing plants won't come without big tax breaks, and the state wasn't interested in helping us with those. When Dick Richmond showed up with the plans for the River Walk project, it was exactly what we've been hoping for."

"Curt, that still doesn't answer my question. Why should the city pay for it?"

Stoneham cleared his throat, and said, "We promised them new roads to the project and to cover all the utility construction, but it wasn't enough to cinch the deal. Come on, Blackie, you know I asked you about it when they proposed the park and staircase. We promised to pursue the eminent domain case to take the property they needed, and to build the staircase and the park. Everything has been first class since we said yes."

The mayor's eyes narrowed. "What are you implying, Curt?"

Stoneham knew he was on dangerous ground. "Nothing, Mr. Mayor, just that they paid for all of our trips to see similar projects, and we all went on those fishing trips with Dick Richmond, that's all. He's been happy to pay for anything we'd like, and there have been more than a few four-star meals for planning sessions." He paused. "We didn't do anything wrong, exactly, but it sure wouldn't be a good idea to not deliver on getting those properties condemned. If they ended up being excluded from the River Walk project, there could be some serious blowback from it."

Now Mayor Ferguson looked worried. "What kind of blowback?"

"Well, sir, a lot of the big names in town have invested in this project, and they could take some major losses." He didn't have to say that most of them were donors to the mayor's campaigns. "I wouldn't be surprised if some city employees had invested in it, too."

There was an uncomfortable silence in the room, then Dawn heard a chair slide back. She quickly disconnected the open intercom, slid the voice recorder into her drawer, and had her fingers on the computer keyboard as the mayor stuck his head into her office.

"Dawn, did you get ahold of Dick Richmond?"

"Yes sir, he'll be here at four o'clock." She was hoping he didn't notice the perspiration under the arms of her dark blouse.

"Send him in as soon as he gets here."

Ferguson returned to his office as Curt Stoneham walked out, looking pale and nervous. He didn't speak to her as he left.

Chapter Nineteen

When Dick Richmond left his office to drive over to city hall, he was on top of the world. His firm had recently broken ground on the River Walk development, and the new Mercedes he was driving was a little gift to himself, an early celebration of the fat pot of money that was coming his way from investors in the sprawling complex. As he drove by the rising construction cranes, he thought about how many years it had taken to get here.

He'd done plenty of smaller commercial development projects over the decades, hampered only by occasional dips in the economy and the never-ending need to raise money. Raising money meant promising healthy returns to investors, and he'd been pretty good at delivering on that promise. This one was his crowning achievement. It would rise over the sleepy river like a modern day castle, glass towers at its peak instead of battlements.

And he'd be the king. The one they turned to in this part

of Florida when a city wanted a signature project to raise its fortunes. All of the pieces were falling into place. All except one. His good mood evaporated as he thought about the slow pace of the eminent domain case. The bad press was making the judge hesitant to hand a victory to him too quickly, and he was getting impatient. Richmond wanted those ratty buildings gone, swept away to give him a clean slate to build his vision on.

He'd paid good money to make it happen, and if there's one thing he hated, it was a politician who didn't stay bought.

Richmond was all smiles as he entered the office. "Hi Dawn, I take it hizzoner is waiting for me?"

"Yes sir, he told me to have you go right in."

The mayor looked up as the door opened, and jumped up to shake his hand. "Dick, good to see you. Everything going well with the construction?"

Richmond took a seat across from the mayor's desk. "Yes, it's moving right along. The foundations are poured on the first two buildings and two of the construction cranes will be finished by the end of the week."

"Good, good, glad to hear that." Silence followed.

"Blackie, you asked for this meeting, what's up?"

The mayor leaned back in his chair, and said, "I'm a little worried about the eminent domain case."

"What's there to worry about? You told me it was an open and shut case."

"The judge will side with us, it's a legitimate public use of the property. That's not the problem."

"Then what is the problem?"

"We're getting a lot of heat in the media, and we've come off looking like the bad guys, taking away mom and pop businesses to give the land away."

"Blackie, you knew going in that those people were going to get the short end of the stick. There's winners and losers in every project, and they were in the middle of where we needed to build. That makes them the losers."

"Look, Dick, it's bad public relations, that's all. I was hoping we could come up with a compromise, maybe sweeten the pot a little."

"Fine with me, Blackie. You can give them whatever you want."

"The mayor looked relieved. "That's very generous of you, Dick. I was thinking that if we could bump up the offer on the properties by a few hundred thousand dollars, it would smooth things over a lot."

Richmond cast flinty eyes at Ferguson. "Why does that make me generous?"

"Well, um, I was thinking that Dolphin River Partners could help with the extra money."

Laughing, Richmond said, "That's a good one, Blackie!"

The mayor looked grim. "I'm serious."

Dick Richmond sat tall in his chair and leaned forward. "Explain to me why I would give you money to help build a public park in the middle of my $65 million dollar project."

"Come on now, Dick, you know we've spent millions putting in new roads and utilities for the River Walk. We had to issue bonds to pay for it, and the city's going to be tight on funds until this all starts to deliver on the tax rolls."

"Sounds like bad financial planning by the city fathers to me."

Ferguson's face turned purple. "That's bullshit and you know it. You sold me on this deal with the promise of great things for Dolphin River, not financial problems. You said if the city could deliver that land, that we'd all make out well."

Richmond leaned back in his chair, interlaced his fingers as he put his arms on his knee, and spoke with quiet malevolence. "Some of us have. I believe you are one of them, Mr. Mayor."

"Damn it, Dick, you know what I mean. The city is tapped out until the end of the fiscal year. I need you to help us get this eminent domain thing wrapped up."

Richmond stood up and leaned both arms on Ferguson's desk. "We had a deal, and I expect the city to honor it. How you pay for it is your problem." He turned on his heel and walked out of the office.

Dawn DeLuca had been too nervous to try the intercom recording a second time, but with her ear against the door she had heard most of what the loud voices had to say. This was worse than she thought. She badly wanted to talk to Andy Mays, but where was he?

She was startled out of her thoughts when the mayor stuck his head out of his office door. He looked somber as he spoke to Dawn. "Tell Jim Watson to come to my office." He retreated back to his desk, sat down heavily, and thought about how he would approach the problem with the city attorney. Watson was a straight shooter, and he was already uncomfortable about the negotiations with the property owners in the eminent domain case.

His intercom buzzed. "Mayor Ferguson, Mr. Watson is here to see you."

"Send him in."

The city attorney was all business. "Good afternoon, Mr. Mayor, what can I do for you?"

"Sit down, Jim. I'd like to talk about how the negotiations are going on the eminent domain case."

Watson gave a grimace, and said, "They aren't going at all. Those folks are waiting for a better deal than what's on the table. Frankly, sir, I think we should raise our offer."

"Jim, I wish we could do that, but there just isn't any money to increase it right now. We've spent so much on the infrastructure improvements that we don't have any more money to give them."

"Well, Mr. Mayor, I know that the judge is a friend of yours, but we always knew our initial offer was on the low side. If this thing goes to court, he's liable to increase the amount the city pays for the property."

"If he does, can we appeal it?"

"Yes, but unless it's a really big number, we're likely to lose. The judge will use land sales values to set the price, but I don't think he's going to buy our argument that the businesses on the property have no real worth except for the land. We could get stung on this thing if we don't increase the offer."

Mayor Ferguson looked glum. "The city doesn't have the money, at least not until the next fiscal year. Could we offer them deferred payments?" It was a tactic that worked at the used car lot he owned.

Watson seemed startled by the suggestion. "Blackie, do you want my honest opinion about the best way to handle this?"

The mayor reluctantly nodded yes.

"I think we should drop the eminent domain and let those businesses stay right where they are. The city had no good reason to kick them out in the first place, and now we can't even afford to pay them a fair price. I say let this park and staircase idea die."

"I'm sorry Jim, I can't agree to that."

Watson stood up and straightened his suit coat. "Mayor Ferguson, I'm an attorney, not a magician. Whatever happens with this case, don't say I didn't warn you."

Dawn Deluca scrambled back to her desk as the city attorney left the mayor's office, stunned by what she'd heard through the door. This kept getting worse. She knew a lot more about what was going on than she wanted, but there was no one she felt safe talking to. She needed Andy Mays.

§

I felt like I was running out of time, and out of ways to fight the city's land grab. I'd managed to get enough of Mardy Jackson's victims to sign on to the lawsuit that Walter was eager to move forward with it. The suit would do a lot to stop Jackson, but it was unlikely to do any more than embarrass the city, and it wouldn't stop them from bulldozing Sandy's marina. I needed another witness now that Andy Mays was gone, but I couldn't forget that talking to me got him killed. I'd have to be careful.

Andy had said that Dawn DeLuca knew about his

concerns, and he believed that she had copies of many of the same travel expense receipts that he kept locked in his safe. All I had to do was get her to talk to Walter, but without putting her in the crosshairs. Not an easy task. Deciding that a bold approach would work better than trying to find her at home, I wrote her a note. It said, "Call me on your cell phone when you are off work. It's about Andy Mays."

It made me feel a little guilty, because I knew it would make her think I had information about Andy, and what I knew, I could never tell her. I signed the note and added my phone number, then folded it small with tucked in edges, like we used to do in middle school. I drove to city hall and took the elevator to the mayor's office. He wasn't likely to be in this late in the day, but that was the point of my visit. I walked into the reception area, and Dawn was at her desk.

"Hi Dawn, is the mayor in?"

"No, Mr. Harper, he's not. Did you have an appointment?" She looked skeptical.

"Not really, I just hoped I'd catch him in. Can you see if he has time to see me in the morning?"

"Honestly, Mr. Harper, I don't think he wants to talk to you."

I moved closer to the desk. "Humor me, check his calendar, OK?"

She looked on her computer screen, and as she did I looked around quickly to be sure no one was within sight of her desk. When she looked up I put a finger against my lips to warn her to be silent, and slipped the folded note across the desk to her.

She resumed talking without a hitch, but I could see fear in her eyes as she palmed the message.

"I'm sorry, Mr. Harper, but the mayor has a very full schedule this week. Perhaps you could check back another time."

"Oh well, at least I tried. Tell Mayor Ferguson he can't avoid me forever."

"I'll tell him, sir."

Her pale face left me wondering if she'd respond to the note, or if she'd join the ranks of people avoiding me. I'd just have to wait to find out.

Chapter Twenty

A couple of days had gone by, and I still had no phone call from Dawn DeLuca. It was beginning to look like another dead end unless something happened to change her mind. Until then, I'd have to keep looking for evidence on my own.

Captain Rick saw me drinking coffee on the deck of the WanderLust as he roamed the docks, and called up to me. "Morning, Will, got any more of that coffee you could share?"

"Sure, come aboard." I stepped into the galley, poured a mug for him and took it to where he'd made himself comfortable in a deck chair.

"Thanks." He took a sip, and said, "Two sugars, just the way I like it."

"What brings you by on a sunny morning like this? With this weather, I'd expect you to be out fishing."

He looked at me over the rim of the cup, drank some

more, and said, "Guess you haven't heard that a storm is coming."

That was hard to imagine with the beautiful weather we were enjoying at the moment, but boaters seldom joke about storms. "No, I've been busy with other things, so I haven't been checking the forecast. What's up?"

"Tropical storm Mindy. Not likely to make it to hurricane winds, but the forecast is for it to enter the Gulf of Mexico day after tomorrow. I'm doubling up the lines on the Waxing Gibbous, and you'd be wise to do the same."

There had been a few mild blows since I'd taken up residence on my boat at the SailFin Point Marina, but this was the first significant storm. "Rick, you know a lot more about riding out the weather on a boat than I do. Is it normal to stay at the dock? I've read about people moving their boats to hurricane holes for safety."

He chuckled and said "We're far enough inland here to be in pretty good shape unless it's a lot bigger storm than this one looks to be. The Bradenton area hasn't been hit by very many big storms over the years, so we're fairly safe here. The Dolphin River Marina is even farther inland, and as long as they have everything tied down, Sandy should be in good shape, too. The main thing is not to leave anything loose on your deck that could go flying, and to double your lines so they don't stretch in the wind and let the hull beat against the dock. Your boat is tall with a lot of windage, so you'll need stout rope. A little preparation saves a lot of damage."

"Thanks for the tip. I guess the ship's store is the best place to pick up more lines."

"Yes, but you'd better get them today before they sell out." He grinned, and said, "There always seems to be a few newbies who buy their extra dock lines at the last minute."

"Thanks Rick, I get the message. I'll head up there shortly."

We made idle conversation for a few minutes, and he asked me again if I'd heard anything from Andy Mays.

"No, not a thing. I'll let you know if I do." Lying to him felt bad, even if it was by omission, but I didn't feel there was any other choice. Andy had been missing long enough now that I guessed his body was gone forever, lost to the deep. It was probably better that way.

§

After my shopping trip to the marina store, I stowed the lines on board. Tomorrow would be plenty of time to put them in place. Today I had other things to worry about. It had been a few days since I'd talked to Sandy, and I figured she had her hands full repairing damage from the vandalism and keeping the marina limping along. We didn't have the type of relationship where we needed to talk every day, but more than three days without contact was unusual. I'd had nothing but bad news about the eminent domain case and hadn't wanted to run over and share it, but now the coming storm was a good excuse to visit.

I drove the Z4 over to her marina, and found her in the office talking on the phone. I waited patiently outside the door while she finished her call, then stepped inside. "Hey Sandy, everything going OK?"

She gave me a rueful smile, and said "*Come ci come ça.*"

That's French for neither good nor bad, more like so-so, and I knew it meant she was a little down.

"Did you get the skiff running?" The vandalism that left it sunken at the dock was one more expense for her.

She sighed and said, "Yes, but only because the repair shop loaned me an old outboard while they rebuild the damaged one. It sat in the water long enough to need an overhaul."

"I suppose you've heard about the storm headed this way?"

"*Oui*, that's what my phone call was about. The new dock tenants bought all of the heavy lines I had in stock, so I'm getting more shipped in overnight. There always seem to be those who prepare at the last minute." She smiled and said, "Hope you weren't coming here to buy lines for the WanderLust."

"No, I already bought mine." I was tempted to take credit, but I came clean. "To be honest, Captain Rick came by this morning to warn me."

She stood and came around the desk to give me a welcoming hug. "You have a good group of people on your dock, Will. They can help you when you need to know something like that. Boaters are good about helping each other."

"I'm sure I'll need plenty of help along the way. How about you? I guess you are all prepared for the storm."

"Yes, but I'll wait until it's a little closer for the last minute preparations. These storms have a way of turning in unexpected directions, and putting away every loose thing around here is a big job. I don't do it unless I have to."

"Can I help you, Sandy?"

"That would be wonderful. Enrique is a big help, but going up and down every dock to check all of the boats is a chore. Storm damage is not the marina's responsibility, but if a dock tenant leaves a chair out and it blows through my store window, I'm still the one who has to repair it. Not everyone is as prepared as you." She grinned as she said it, and I knew I was being teased for my novice status.

I put my arm around her waist, and said, "We could ride out the storm together."

"That would be lovely, Will, but you need to be on your boat. If a line breaks or a window leaks, you should be there to deal with it."

Busted as a novice again. "Sounds like a good idea. Guess I'll plan on an evening alone when the storm arrives."

"I'd love to have your help tomorrow, though. Why don't you join me here and we'll go to Carol's diner for lunch, then walk the docks together to get them ready for the wind."

I kissed her, and said, "That's a date."

§

Tropical storm Mindy made landfall two days later as predicted, and while the winds were around 50 miles an hour, it didn't last too long. I was glad my introduction to this type of storm wasn't a major hurricane, because I felt a little unprepared as my boat pitched and rocked while straining against the dock lines for several hours. Some things came crashing off of their shelves, and the wine rack dumped several bottles onto the cabin sole in a staining, sticky mess. I couldn't stay on my feet with the boat rocking in the wind to clean it up without risking major cuts from the broken glass, and was forced to throw a couple of dark towels over the pile to keep it from spreading.

The boat banged the dock pilings a few times, but the doubled up lines seemed to do a pretty good job of avoiding major damage. The wind died down around two a.m., and I was finally able to get some sleep. The dawn shining through the cabin window woke me early, and I threw on shorts and a tee shirt to go outside and see how the marina had faired. The WanderLust had a few scrapes on the paint where she'd banged on the dock, but seemed otherwise unscathed. I was glad Captain Rick and Sandy had given me a heads up on the things that could be damaged or blown away, and my preparations seems to have been sufficient.

There was a lot of trash in the water, palm fronds, limbs and debris that usually stays on land such as fast-food wrappers and the occasional old flip-flop, but after walking the docks, no one seemed to have lost much to the storm. I stopped by The Waxing Gibbous, and found Captain Rick on the upper deck, grumbling.

"You do OK in the storm, Rick?"

He walked to the rail and looked down at me. "Nothing big, but the damn wind ripped the plastic out of my flybridge cover." It was the windshield that kept the upper driving station cozy in cold or rainy weather, and it could be an expensive repair.

"Sorry to hear that. At least it's an easy fix."

"Easy, but not cheap. That's a big piece of plastic, and it's been less than a year since I had the new one made." He shook his head. "Hell, I should be happy that's all that happened. Everything OK on your boat?"

"Yes, just a few scrapes where the lines stretched and it bumped the dock."

"Will, as high as that fancy boat of yours sits, you're lucky that's all that happened."

"Believe me, I'm not complaining." I said goodbye and continued my tour of the docks; it looked like SailFin Point had escaped relatively unscathed. I decided I'd better check in with Sandy and see how the Dolphin River Marina had fared in the storm. I dialed her number and said, "Hi, Sandy, how are things at the marina?"

"Pretty good, actually. A few of the dock tenants lost deck chairs and a piece of metal roofing on my storage shed blew off, but that seems to be all so far. Is everything OK on your boat?"

"No real problems, just a few paint scrapes where the hull bumped the dock in the wind."

I could almost see her smile. "I'll show you how to tie the lines where that won't happen next time. Want to come over later and celebrate surviving the storm by sharing a bottle of wine?"

"I'd love to. Is four o'clock good?"

"Lovely. I'll see you then."

§

On Anna Maria Island, the beaches were thick with shell collectors taking advantage of the new batch of often pristine shells, blown onto the sand by the wind and the waves of tropical storm Mindy. The morning after a storm was always crowded on the beach, and today was no exception. Not all the finds were in such perfect condition.

Betsy Thrasher was a hard core shell collector, and she was willing to dig through beach trash that others avoided in search of an elusive specimen. Driftwood, clumps of seaweed and the occasional dead fish or jellyfish kept the less die-hard beachcombers away from the usually smelly, slimy piles of debris, but not Betsy. As she used her walking stick to poke at a particularly large bunch of flotsam, she spotted a flash of white that could be a shell. Pushing the seaweed off of it, she was instead greeted with a skeleton foot.

Andy Mays was back.

Chapter Twenty-One

News of a body washed up on the shore of Anna Maria Island spread fast in the waterfront community. The condition of the remains was extremely poor after weeks in the ocean, but the depressed fracture of the skull that was the cause of death was easy to see. Identification was being withheld awaiting confirmation with dental records, but there was only one person believed missing who fit the size and apparent age of the body. It was Andy Mays.

When I first heard the news on the dock grapevine, I was startled, but managed not to react strangely.

My neighbor Bev hollered across from her boat "Hey Will, did you hear they found a body on Anna Maria Island after the storm? They think it might be that guy who went missing at city hall."

"What happened, did he drown?" I asked her.

"No, it looked like he was hit in the head according to the TV news reports. Some shell collectors found him after the weather blew through."

"That's a shame, I hope they find out what happened to him." I was trying to say the right things, but I was hoping they wouldn't find anything remaining on his body to link him to either Sandy or to me.

"Yeah, me too. I've got to run now, have a good day, Will."

"You too." Somehow I didn't think it was going to be a very good one.

I didn't want to tell Sandy the news over the phone, so I drove over to the Dolphin River Marina to find her. She was busy helping Enrique patch the storm-damaged roof of the storage building when I found her.

"Hey, Will, what brings you over this way?" she asked.

"There's something I wanted to ask you about. Mind if I borrow the boss for a few minutes, Enrique?"

"No problem, Mr. Harper, just bring her back when you're done." He was smiling when he said it, and I guessed they hadn't heard about the grim discovery on the beach.

Sandy climbed down from the roof, gave me a welcoming hug, and said "What's up, Will?"

I took her arm and led her towards the office, where we could sit on the bench at the front. Depending on the time of day it could be filled with tourists enjoying the view or with fisherman sharing stories of the day's catch, but right now it was empty.

She could tell the news wouldn't be good. "What is it?"

I took a deep breath and told her. "A body washed up on Anna Maria Island. They think it's Andy Mays."

She turned pale, and put her head in her hands. "Oh God, this is awful."

I put an arm around her, and said "It might not be. The body is badly decomposed after all this time in the water. It sounds like the only thing they can tell for sure so far is that he was hit in the head with something."

She looked up at me, arms hugging her knees. "What can we do?"

"Nothing but wait. Once the body is positively identified, the police will be checking with everyone who was in contact with him recently, and my calls will show on his phone records. That's the only link to us that I know about."

"What will you tell them?"

"The truth, up to a point. That I was asking him for information about the Eminent Domain case the city is pursuing, and that he said he couldn't help me because he was afraid. Maybe that will get them thinking about who he might have been afraid *of.*"

"I want this to all just go away, Will." She looked miserable, and I wished I could give her the answer she wanted, but it wasn't that easy.

"Stay calm, Sandy, that's all we can do. The good part about them finding Andy is that now the police know he was murdered, that he didn't leave town to run away from the problems. It could put pressure on whoever killed him."

She leaned back, stared at the sky, and sighed. "As long as the police don't think it was us."

That was something we could both agree on.

§

Curt Stoneham heard the news that was buzzing through city hall. Andy Mays' body had been found. Although the identification was still unconfirmed, Stoneham didn't have any doubts that it was him. Worse, he thought he knew who killed him. When he gave Bo Wolf's name to Mardy Jackson, he'd known it was a mistake. He'd been frustrated by all of the pressure he'd gotten from the mayor and those damn reporters over the staircase project for the River Walk, and Bo Wolf was the kind of guy who could make his own pressure to counter it.

Stoneham hadn't counted on Wolf resorting to murder though, and now it connected back to him. Damn. He knew he should stay as far away from Bo as possible, but he needed to tell him to leave town. It was the only way to keep this from blowing up in his face. He debated using a phone in another office, but phone records would link him to Wolf, so that horse was already out of the barn. He closed his door, and made the call.

"Bo, it's Curt. Did you hear that Andy Mays' body washed ashore?"

"Yeah, what difference does that make to me?" Wolf said quietly.

"Uh, just that you'd threatened him. That might make you a suspect."

"You'd better not say that to anyone else."

"No, no, that's not what I meant, Bo. I was just wondering

if it might be a good idea to make yourself scarce until the heat dies down, that's all."

A long silence followed. Stoneham was getting nervous, waiting for an outburst that never came. Finally Wolf spoke.

"Curt, if you want me out of town for awhile, I don't travel cheap. Come to my place tonight at eight p.m., and bring ten grand in cash. Then I'll go for as long as you like."

"Bo! Where am I supposed to get that kind of money? I don't keep that much cash around."

"I know about your safety deposit box, Curt, and I know it's full of cash. You're lucky that's all I'm taking. Argue some more and the price will go up."

Stoneham didn't have any choice. "OK, I'll be there." He hung up the phone. It all felt like it was falling apart. Getting into that deal with Mardy Jackson had been stupid, especially with what he'd already been paid by Dick Richmond for pushing the park and staircase deal through. He'd gotten greedy, and he knew it. It wouldn't be a good idea to show up at Bo Wolf's place unarmed.

§

Meanwhile, Wolf was having the same thought. He'd spent the afternoon digging up his jars full of cash from the yard, then showered the dirt and sweat from his muscled body before packing his things to go. That idiot Stoneham thought he was running him out of town, but Bo had been planning this all along. Stay in one place while the money was good, and when the heat got to be too much... disappear.

The tactic had worked well, and this was the third city

where he had made a bundle when the local power brokers needed someone to do their dirty work. He knew they were always happy to see him go, partly because he knew where the bodies were buried. Literally. This was the first time he had screwed up, trying to get tricky by framing Sandy St. Martin when he left Andy Mays' body on her boat. None of the bodies he'd left behind in the past had ever turned up, and that kept him out of the spotlight. Not this time.

Maybe it was time to take a long vacation in the islands. Not before he dealt with Curt Stoneham and Mardy Jackson though. It was time to show them who was really in charge.

Bo Wolf was sitting on the front steps of his trailer when he saw the lights of Stoneham's sedan pull down the long, gravel drive. He was again cleaning his nails with a long knife, something that he'd noticed made government types very nervous. They were used to subservient underlings, and he was neither. Always good to remind them of that.

Stoneham got out of his car, shut the door, and walked slowly towards the trailer carrying a canvas duffle bag.

"Hey, Bo. I got what you asked for." He glanced at the piles of dirt scattered around, and said "You got a problem with gopher tortoises out here?"

Chuckling, Wolf said, "Yeah, something like that." He paused, then said, "You going to bring that bag over here, or you planning on staying out in the yard?"

He moved a little closer, holding the bag in both hands. "Listen, Bo, after I give you the money, we're good, right? No hard feelings."

"Curt, how could you even ask me that?" His cheshire cat grin did not match his words.

They were twenty feet apart, like a pair of gunfighters in the old west, wondering who would make the first move. "So you'll take the money and leave like you said?"

"Sure, Curt. Now just bring it over here so I can make sure it's all there."

Hesitantly, Stoneham walked toward the rickety porch. He stopped several feet short, and dropped the bag at Wolf's feet. "There it is. Now you can afford to leave."

There was no pretense of a smile on Bo Wolf's face now. "Curt, you're really starting to piss me off, you know? I could always *afford* to leave, I just wanted a little extra *inspiration*, that's all. He reached for the bag, and said "Let's see how inspired I'm going to be."

As he unzipped the bag, Stoneham reached into his waistband and pulled out a gun. "Bo, the money's all there like I said it would be. But before you leave, I want those papers that you took from Andy Mays."

Wolf looked up in surprise at the gun, shaking in Stoneham's hand as he pointed it at his chest. He set the bag full of cash down, put his hand in the air and said, "Curt, you have more balls than I ever gave you credit for, but you are sorely lacking in brains to go with them. Do you really think I'd keep those papers sitting around my house for anyone to find?"

"Where did you put them, then?"

"Curt, Curt, Curt. Where would I be if I let every bozo with a gun tell me what to do? Why, I'd have no reputation at all.

Then I'd be out of business, and we can't have that, can we?"

Stoneham's pale face glowed in the moonlight, eyes wide as he listened to his death sentence. "Don't make me shoot you, Bo."

With lightning speed Wolf threw his body sideways, grabbed the knife and threw it at Curt Stoneham as the gun roared in his ear. He leapt at Stoneham and grabbed the gun from his hand as they both went down, rolling away and jumping to his feet. Curt Stoneham was on the ground, the knife buried to the hilt in his shoulder, groaning as his eyes widened in shock. Wolf brushed the dirt from his clothes as he looked at the bleeding man on the ground.

"Curt, I lied, you know. Those papers are hidden in the attic." He lifted the revolver, pointed it at Stoneham's bulging eyes, and shot him in the head. He examined the carnage as the smoke cleared. "Well look at that. You have more brains than I thought."

Chapter Twenty-Two

Bo Wolf wasn't about to make the same mistake twice. He dragged Curt Stoneham's body into the brush behind his trailer and buried it, then used a shovel to clean up the spot where the murder had taken place. Stoneham would be missed more quickly than Andy Mays had been, so the time for Wolf's departure was running short.

He packed a bag with a few clothes, and took everything out to his pickup truck. The toolbox in the bed of the truck had a false bottom with a recess welded into the frame of the truck bed, and he packed the duffle with Curt's cash and the rest of the money he'd dug up from the yard. It was a tight fit, but he wasn't about to leave any of his hard-earned cash behind.

As he drove away from the trailer, he grinned in anticipation of his next stop. Mardy Jackson.

§

Dawn DeLuca was in a panic. She'd heard the news of the discovery of Andy Mays' remains on the beach, and she didn't know what to do about it. She'd wanted to believe that he'd run away, but now there was no hiding from the truth. Her friend was dead. Murdered. And he was likely dead because of what he knew about the city's involvement in the River Walk project. The same things she knew.

She'd tried all evening to get Curt Stoneham on the phone, going so far as risking a call to his house. When his wife answered, Dawn had hung up.

Maybe it was time to call that reporter, Will Harper.

She dialed the number on the folded note. "Hello, Mr. Harper? It's Dawn DeLuca. I think I'm in trouble."

"Dawn, you're in more than just trouble. I want to help you, but you have to trust me. And call me Will."

"OK, Will, I heard that Andy Mays is dead, and now Curt is missing too. I'm scared."

"Curt Stoneham? I didn't know that. What's his connection?"

She hesitated, and said "Can we talk about this in person?" Admitting her affair to a stranger wasn't easy, but she knew she'd have to come clean.

"Where are you now, Dawn?"

"I'm at home, my apartment I mean."

"OK, pack a bag with what you need for a couple of days, and we'll hide you in a hotel. This has gotten dangerous, and if you have the information I think you do, someone may want to keep you quiet. What's your address?"

Too scared to argue, she gave the address and apartment number to him.

"I'll be there in twenty minutes. Do you remember what I look like from seeing me in the mayor's office?"

"Yes."

"Good, look through your peephole, and don't open the door to anyone but me."

"OK." She hung up the phone, and a chill passed through her. There was no turning back now.

Twenty minutes later, she was sitting near the door, bag packed, waiting for Will Harper. She heard the car pull up outside, but still managed to be startled when the doorbell rang. She looked through the peephole, and saw the familiar face. Opening the door for him, she stepped back as he slipped inside the dimly-lit apartment.

"Are you ready, Dawn?"

"Yes, my clothes are in this bag." She lifted the canvas shoulder bag next to it, and said, "This is everything I have about the River Walk development."

I picked up her bag. "That's the smartest thing you can do. Get the evidence out there before they know you have it." I walked her to my car, put her bag in the trunk, helped her into the low-slung seat, and we drove to what I hoped would be a safe hiding place. I'd already rented a room in my name at a small beach motel in Bradenton, the kind where they rent by the week and still have paper records. The rooms had seen thousands of Northern visitors over the years and had a fair amount of wear, but were clean and well-kept.

When we arrived, I got her bag and walked her to the door, unlocking it and stepping aside as she entered. "It's not fancy, but you should be safe here. May I come in and talk for a bit?"

"Sure." Dawn took her bag and set it on the edge of the double bed, unzipped a side compartment and pulled out a bottle of red wine and a corkscrew. "Would you open this and I'll look for glasses?"

I didn't want to drink much, but I could tell she needed to calm her nerves before telling me her story. The cork came out with a 'pop', and she returned with a pair of glass tumblers wrapped in paper covers with the motel logo on the side. I hadn't seen motel glasses presented that way in years, and the nostalgia brought a smile to my face. I pulled mine out of the cover and held it up to the light. "A few scratches, but clean, just like the rest of this place. My parents brought me to Florida a few times when I was growing up, and we stayed in places just like this."

She gave me a small smile in return, and held her glass up for me to fill. We sat at a round table by the window with the drapes closed, took a sip of the wine, and she began her story. "When Dick Richmond first showed up at city hall with his proposal for the River Walk, we were all so excited. I grew up near Dolphin River, and I'd watched it go down hill while places like Bradenton seemed to get bigger all the time. The development was going to put our little town on the map, and I didn't see that there could be anything bad about that. The mayor's whole staff worked with Dolphin River Partners to put the land together, and we were all sworn to secrecy. I guess that's when I got involved with Curt Stoneham."

"Involved?"

She sighed. 'We spent a lot of time together because I was arranging the trips for the economic development team to tour similar projects around the country. DRP paid for all of it, and I wondered if that was ethical, but Mayor Ferguson told me not to worry about it. He said he was trying to save the city money, and that sounded reasonable. Anyway, Curt and I were flirting, I was lonely, and we had an affair." She bit her lip. "I guess you'd say we still are, but there hasn't been much time to be together since the eminent domain case blew up."

"What do you mean, 'blew up'?"

"When Mr. Richmond first proposed the park and staircase in the middle of the River Walk, Curt and the planning department went right along with the idea. Andy was the only one who said it was a mistake."

"Andy Mays?"

"Yes, he tried to get Curt and the mayor to consider working the marina, diner, and the bait shack into the project, but he got shot down. He even showed how much money it would save, and did some rough sketches of ways to put new fronts on the buildings to give it an 'old Florida' look while still fitting in with the new buildings. Curt told him to drop it or get fired, and I'm not sure the mayor ever even looked at the sketches." She picked up her canvas bag, and said "I made copies, do you want to see them?"

"I'd love to."

Dawn pulled the folded sketches out of her bag and

smoothed them as she put them on the table between us. "Aren't they wonderful?"

And they were. The tin-roofed porches adorning the colorful buildings were flanked by palm trees, and they looked like they'd be right at home in Key West. It was easy to see how they would be an asset to the River Walk. "Andy did a beautiful job with this. Why was Curt so opposed to the idea?"

"Because it wasn't what Dick Richmond and Dolphin River Partners wanted. I'm not supposed to know this, but Richmond sold shares in the development to most of the people with money in town, and several people in city hall bought shares too. I heard him telling Blackie that he could buy in at a discount in return for the city's help with the project."

This was just the kind of smoking gun I was looking for. "Do you have any of that in writing?"

"No, Curt and the mayor were careful to keep that kind of paperwork from me. What I have is the travel documents for their trips, receipts for fancy meals and hotels, that sort of thing."

I couldn't keep the disappointment off my face. "That could help, but I don't know if it would be enough for the judge to stop the eminent domain."

"There is one more thing." Dawn reached in the bag and pulled out the small recorder. "I taped Curt talking to the mayor about promising Dick Richmond that the city would take those buildings for the staircase and park." She pressed play, and the booming voice of Mayor Blackie Ferguson filled the room, talking to Curt Stoneham about why the city should pay for Dolphin River Partners amenities. When Curt answered him on the recording, Will Harper thought it might be enough.

Through the hollow sound of the intercom, Stoneham said "We promised them new roads to the project and to cover all the utility construction, but it wasn't enough to cinch the deal. Come on Blackie, you know I asked you about it when they proposed the park and staircase. We promised to pursue the eminent domain case to take the property they needed, and to build the staircase and the park. Everything has been first class since we said yes."

Will leaned back in his chair and took a sip of his wine as the recording ended. "This proves that Dick Richmond and DRP asked the city to get rid of the buildings and take the land for that park. It might not be admissible as evidence, but if I can arrange for the judge to hear it somehow, he'd have a hard time siding with the city."

Dawn bit her nails nervously. "They'll know it came from me."

"Let me talk to our attorney, Walter Lord. If he could get you whistle-blower status, you'd be protected against being fired."

"Getting fired was what Andy was worried about at first. Now he's dead."

I put my hand on top of hers on the table. "Dawn, I'm going to do my best to protect you, starting with having Walter get someone to take a deposition of what you've told me. You can testify to having heard the conversation as it was being recorded, too. The more we can get on the record, the less reason anyone will have to go after you. I'll take your documents and drawings as well, and get them to Walter. They'll be safe with him."

"What will happen to Curt?"

"He might go to jail for accepting a bribe. We'll have to see how it all shakes out."

She looked miserable. "This will be awful for his wife. She's going to find out about us, won't she?"

"You can't worry about that now. Keeping you safe is what's important." I didn't want to say it, but I was more worried about keeping Dawn DeLuca alive.

Chapter Twenty-Three

Mayor Blackie Ferguson was pissed. When he'd arrived at his city hall office this morning, he'd expected his secretary, Dawn DeLuca, to be waiting with his morning coffee and copies of the area newspapers that he usually had her pick up on her way in. Instead, the office door was locked, and when he dug his keys out and let himself in, it was dark and deserted. He thought, *She'd better have a damn good excuse for this*. She had always been reliable, but she'd been a little shaky since Andy Mays' disappearance. He suspected the news of his body washing up on the beach was the reason for her absence.

Well dammit, if she needs a personal day she should call and ask first. He turned on the lights in his office, sat at his desk, and was about to buzz Dawn and ask her to get Curt Stoneham on the line when he remembered she wasn't there. *Crap*. Dialing Curt's direct line himself, he let the phone ring eight times before he hung up and called the switchboard. "Diane, get the City Planners Office on the phone for me. Not Curt, his secretary, what's her name? OK, then get Denice on the phone."

He waited without much patience as the phone rang. "Hey, Denice? Is Curt around the office somewhere?"

"No sir, could I leave a message for him?"

He fumed silently. "This is Mayor Ferguson. Have him call me the minute he gets in."

"Yes sir, I'll be sure to tell him."

I really need to talk to him about this Andy Mays thing. Having the decomposed bodies of city employees washing up on the local beaches wasn't good for anybody, and he wanted to make sure no one in city hall had anything to do with it. He'd heard rumors in the building about Curt Stoneham being seen with Bo Wolf, and that guy was a loose cannon for sure. *I sure hope Curt hasn't let him do something stupid.*

§

Bo Wolf was pretty damn pissed too. He'd spent half the night trying to find Mardy Jackson, and no one seemed to know where he was. He'd been to his house, his office and to every bar in town looking for him, but no luck. Wolf was tempted to give up and leave town before he became a 'person of interest' to the police, but he hated to go without the money he intended to beat out of Mardy Jackson. Mardy had treated him like an employee, and Bo Wolf didn't take orders from anyone.

Curt Stoneham found that out the hard way. Now it was Jackson's turn.

§

I'd slept in this morning, worn out from the evening spent hiding and questioning Dawn DeLuca, and was now having coffee on the upper deck of the WanderLust. It looked like it would be another beautiful Florida day until I saw the man in a gray golf shirt and slacks walking down the dock with his eye on me. He stopped beside my boat, and called up to me.

"Good morning, are you Will Harper?"

"That depends, what are you selling?" I thought a little humor couldn't hurt, but he didn't seem in the mood for it.

The man held up his badge. "Ray Sheppard, I'm a detective with the Manatee County Sheriff's Department. I've got a few questions for you."

"OK, come aboard." He made his way up the ladder to the upper deck, and I offered him a chair. "Would you like a cup of coffee? I just made a pot."

"No thanks, this shouldn't take long."

That sounded good to me. "What can I do for you, detective?"

"We're investigating the death of Andy Mays, and we discovered several phone calls from your cell phone to his phone in the days before his disappearance. Want to tell me what that was about?"

I'd been expecting this and was prepared. "Yes, I'd been trying to recruit him to help me with the eminent domain case the city of Dolphin River has been pursuing against three businesses on the waterfront."

"And did Mr. Mays agree to help you?"

"No, I'm sorry to say he refused. He said he was afraid

he'd lose his job."

"Did he indicate that he felt like he was in any danger?"

"He did say he'd been kind of indirectly threatened by a guy named Bo Wolf, who appears to work for Curt Stoneham at the Dolphin River City Planners Office."

"What exactly did he say, Mr. Harper?"

"Just that this Wolf character told him there were lots of ways for him to get hurt." I thought I'd better avoid bringing up the threat to frame him with a bogus payoff account, since I had no proof of it.

"When was the last time you saw Andy Mays?"

"I only met him in person once and that was on the playground behind the school a few weeks before he disappeared."

Detective Sheppard raised a bushy eyebrow at that. "Why on the playground? Seems like an odd place to meet."

"I thought so too, but he was worried about anyone seeing us together, so that's the place he picked."

"Is there anything else you can think of that might help us find out who killed Mays?"

"No, I'm sorry, I wish there was. He seemed like a nice young guy." I stopped there, and stayed mute as the detective stared at me, waiting to see if I'd add anything. I'd learned a long time ago in my news career that filling a silence was never a good idea, so I sat quietly and sipped my coffee.

He stood and extended his hand. I shook it, and he said, "Please let us know if you think of anything else that might help our investigation."

"I certainly will, Detective, I hope you find out who did it."

He looked intently at me, and said, "Oh, we'll find him. You can count on that." He made his way down the ladder, onto the dock and back up towards the parking lot. I didn't breathe easy until he was out of sight.

I'd told him the truth, but with a couple of details left out. That night on the playground was the last time I'd seen Andy Mays *alive*.

§

Visiting Sandy was on my list for today, but first I thought I'd better check on Dawn DeLuca. Sitting alone in a motel wasn't much fun, and I worried she might decide that leaving town was a safer bet. I needed her to testify about city hall's cozy relationship with Dolphin River Partners, and keeping her under wraps was the only way to be sure that would happen. I gave her a call.

"Dawn, this is Will Harper. How are you doing?"

"I'm OK, just sick of this room. I went and sat on the beach while they cleaned this morning, but I've been afraid to go anywhere else, and I don't have a car."

"Would you like me to come take you out to lunch?"

"Oh, that would be great. Anything to get out of here for a while."

"I know a great little seafood shack in Bradenton, does that sound good to you?"

"It sounds wonderful."

"I'll pick you up in about an hour. Remember, don't open

the door to anyone but me."

"OK, thanks, Will. I appreciate what you're doing for me."

I said goodbye, pressed the button to end the call, then phoned Sandy.

"Allo?"

"Hi, Sandy, it's Will. How are things at the marina today?"

"Pretty good, actually. Enrique and I have cleaned up and repaired most of the storm damage, and I rented a slip to someone whose dock at one of the Bradenton marinas was beaten up by the high winds. He decided being further inland was safer. His first month's rent and deposit is more than enough to pay for rebuilding the motor on the skiff that was vandalized, and the insurance company sounds like they'll pay for it too, after the deductible."

I smiled, and said, "It's good to hear you sounding more positive."

"I'm trying, Will. How are things going with the fight against the city?"

"Why don't I come over this afternoon and fill you in? It's probably best not to say too much over the phone."

"OK. You've been pampering me a lot lately, why don't I make dinner for us on my boat tonight?"

"As long as I can have the dessert of my choice."

"Will, you are naughty! Don't think I don't know what you want."

"Hey, I'm, just thinking of you. It's a very easy dish to prepare."

She laughed, and said, "I'll see you this afternoon. Bring an appetite."

I'd have no trouble doing that.

§

On the way to pick up Dawn for lunch, I stopped at a Fedex store, made copies of all of her documents, and shipped the originals overnight to Walter Lord. I felt better having them out of my hands, and knew that Walter could use them to help our case. Making sure that Dawn was around to testify would be the key. I locked the copies in my trunk and drove the rest of the way to her hideaway. I'd been keeping an eye out for tails out of an abundance of caution, and hadn't seen any suspicious cars.

I parked a few doors down from her room, strolled down the covered walkway and knocked on her door. I saw the light of the peephole go dark, and she opened the door a crack.

"Hi, Will, come in."

The curtains were closed and the room was dim, a lamp by the bed the only light, a book lying open beside it.

"You ready to get out of here for awhile?"

She was wearing a sundress and sandals, looking even younger than the mid twenties I knew her to be. She grabbed her purse, held it up, and said, "Yes please, get me out of here."

We walked to my car and I held her door for her. When I slid behind the wheel, I said, "Would you like the top down?"

"Oh, that would be wonderful. I want some sun." She marveled at the way the hard top of the BMW folded in on itself before stowing automatically in the trunk, twenty seconds from start to finish. "That's almost like a magic trick!"

Grinning, I said, "It's one of the reasons I bought this car. Sunshine at the push of a button."

Dawn put on her sunglasses, leaned back in the seat and turned her face to the warmth of the sun as I drove us from the beach towards the restaurant. We pulled into the parking lot of the Bridge Tender Inn, and she was delighted at the view as I led her to the patio bar on the waterfront. "Will, this is wonderful. I'm so glad to be outdoors."

We were shown to our seats, ordered a beer for me and white wine for her, and looked over the menu. A dog sitting at the next table wandered over to nuzzle my hand, and I said, "This is one of things I like about this place, the old Florida beachfront atmosphere. Did you notice they even have a Doggie Burger on the menu?"

"That is so funny." Our drinks arrived, and we took a sip before she looked wistfully at me. "You know, this is exactly the kind of atmosphere that Andy envisioned for the diner on the River Walk. The developer wants all fancy chain restaurants, but Andy thought having something like this would be great for everyone."

"I wish they'd listened to him, Dawn. Having a place with character on the Dolphin River would have been wonderful." We lapsed into silence, both of us aware that we weren't far from where Andy's body had washed ashore in the storm. "I sent all of your documents to our attorney. They'll be safe with him."

My statement jolted her back into the present. "That's good. I'm still pretty nervous about all this." She leaned in and spoke softly. "I mean, it got Andy killed."

"That's why we're being careful. I think the police are on the trail of his killer." I told her about my visit from the detective this morning and about passing along my suspicions about Bo Wolf.

"I heard Curt mention his name once, but when I asked who he was, he wouldn't say. Do you think he killed Andy?"

"He's the most likely culprit so far. At least the cops are looking for him."

Our food arrived, and we changed the subject, eager to avoid spoiling our appetites. I'd ordered the blackened grouper sandwich, and Dawn had the Cuban sandwich with black bean soup. Lunch was delicious, and we ordered another round of drinks as we cleaned our plates.

The drinks arrived and Dawn patted her lips, took another sip of her chardonnay, and looked at me across the table. "Do you think Bo Wolf is looking for me?"

"I don't know, but getting your testimony on the record quickly is the best way to protect you. Walter was planning to set up a deposition with a court reporter tomorrow. I'll let you know what the plan is."

She put her hand on mine, and said, "Thank you for keeping me safe, and for taking me out today. It means a lot to me."

I felt my ears turning red and pulled my fingers from hers, patted her wrist with what I hoped felt like comfort from a friend, and tucked my arms safely back under the table. This was a complication I didn't need.

Chapter Twenty-Four

I quickly ended my lunch with Dawn DeLuca, anxious to avoid any problems. She hadn't exactly made a move on me, but seeing me as her protector could certainly lead to a misunderstanding, and I didn't need that. I drove us back to the motel, walked her to the door, and waited as she unlocked it.

"Thank you again, Will. Would you like to stay for a while?"

She looked hopeful, but I knew it would be a mistake. "Sorry, but I have other work to do today. I'll call you with the details on the deposition tomorrow. Stay out of sight, OK?"

She sighed and looked disappointed. "There's a pizza place down the street, I'll order in dinner."

"That's a good idea, I'll talk to you later." She closed the door and I walked away, taking a deep breath.

§

Our attorney, Walter Lord, called as I drove back across towards Bradenton. "Will? It's Walter, I wanted to update you on things with the court case."

"How is it going?"

"No progress on the eminent domain, I'm afraid. The city still won't budge, and the judge is preparing to hold a hearing to gather evidence to set property values. I've arranged everything for Dawn's deposition tomorrow, can you write the address down?"

"Actually, I'm driving at the moment, could you e-mail the details to me?"

"No problem, I'll send them as soon as we get off the phone. I've filed the suit in state court against Mardy Jackson, but so far we haven't been able to locate him to serve the papers. Could you help with that?"

"Sure, what can I do?"

"Go to the courthouse and do a search for his name in the property records. I could do it here, but it will save money on the paralegal if you could handle it."

"Anything specific I'm looking for? He buys and sells real-estate, so he probably has a bunch of transactions."

"Look for property that's not near Dolphin River, maybe a place an hour or two out of town. The process server I use is pretty good, and he says Jackson hasn't been seen in town for days. He may have a weekend place he uses too. It makes me wonder who he's hiding from."

"OK, I'll head over to the courthouse now, and let you know what I find."

"Thanks, Will. It may not stop the eminent domain case, but it's one more way to keep pressure on the city."

I was hoping the public disapproval would start to weigh on the mayor, but so far he hadn't budged.

It was after two and I'd hoped to be at Sandy's by now, but Walter's request didn't sound like it could wait. The courthouse was on the way to her marina, so I stopped, parked in one of the visitor spots and went to the property records office. The staff was usually helpful, but I declined their assistance and went straight to the computer terminals to search on my own. I didn't want my scrutiny of Mardy Jackson's properties ringing any alarm bells in the mayor's office.

There were dozens of transactions in Mardy Jackson's name, and it was a tedious process to track down the addresses of all of them. One advantage I had was that I was familiar with the thirty-seven houses and lots that Jackson had purchased near the River Walk site, and could exclude them pretty quickly. I feared that if he had a weekend place outside of the county that I wouldn't find it in the records, but Manatee County is a big area. Luck was with me, and I found a purchase five years earlier of a small cabin on a lake, surrounded by twelve acres in the middle of nowhere. It was near the Myakka River State Park, about an hour's drive from Dolphin River.

It looked like I might have found Mardy Jackson's hideout.

I called Walter to fill him in on my discovery, and he was pleased. "Good work, Will. Can I ask one more favor?"

"You're the one doing the biggest favor for Sandy and the

three businesses, how can I help?"

"Run by the process server's office and pick up the papers on the lawsuit from Ed Healey. I'd prefer that you be the one to give them to Mardy Jackson in person."

It was after three p.m. already, and this was going to make me very late getting to Sandy's. I didn't feel I could say no to Walter, though. After all, this was being done on Sandy's behalf. "OK, I'll do it."

"Thanks, Will. Be sure you place the papers in his hand. And listen, he's probably beginning to feel pushed into a corner. Be careful, OK?"

"Trust me, I'll watch my back." I'd been doing more of that than he realized lately.

I walked over to the process server's office to get the papers, and Ed seemed glad to be rid of them. "We've been chasing Mardy Jackson all over this town with no luck. Hope you have better success."

"Thanks, Ed, I'm counting on it."

I went to my car, tossed the papers on the front seat, and began the long drive to where I hoped to find Jackson and get him served on the lawsuit over his land purchases. I called Sandy on the way to tell her I'd be arriving closer to dinnertime, and she sounded disappointed.

"Will, I thought you were coming after lunch? Every time I hear a car in the parking lot I think it's you. Why are you so late?"

"Sorry, Sandy, I'm working on something for Walter that came up at the last minute. It's to help your case, so I didn't think

I could turn him down, OK?"

She sighed, and said, "I understand. I was anxious to see you, that's all."

"So am I, sweetie. I can stay as long as you like when I get there."

"Better bring a toothbrush then."

I liked the sound of that.

Between the conversation with Sandy and driving a stick shift through town, I hadn't paid any attention to my rear view mirror. If I had, I might have noticed an older dark-green Ford pickup truck with tinted windows taking the same route. Bo Wolf was on my tail.

§

Following a car on Florida state road 70 into the scrublands of Manatee County without being seen was a challenge, but Wolf had done this before. It had been a spur of the moment decision when he'd spotted Will Harper leaving the courthouse, but he'd gotten tired of driving around looking for Mardy Jackson. Harper had been a pain in the ass over the River Walk project, and Bo would be happy to ruin his day.

Good thing I have a full tank of gas, he thought as he saw the black sports car turn onto Myakka City Road. There was a lot of nothing out this way. Maybe Harper had spotted the truck in his rearview. *I wonder if he's leading me on a wild-goose chase.* Forty minutes out on this barren road, Wolf was about to give up and turn around when he spotted the turn signal on the BMW in the distance. He continued past the turn, noting that it was Sugarbowl Rd. Taking the next opportunity, he pulled a u-turn, drove slowly back to the turnoff, and pulled onto the narrow roadway. It would be tricky trying to keep the little black sports car in sight without getting spotted himself, but this chase was starting to get interesting.

Wolf rounded a corner and was startled to see the car he was following sitting in a driveway in front of a locked gate. He continued past the drive, rounded the next corner, and pulled off the road. *Now what is this about?* He waited a few minutes, then drove back towards the place the BMW had pulled off. The car was empty, and there was no sight of Will Harper. Looking around, he spotted an old barn across the road with a weed covered drive leading to it. He drove his truck slowly down the path to the barn and parked behind it. *Looks like whoever that driveway belongs to isn't expecting company.* He could be patient when it was necessary. This was one of those times.

§

I climbed the short barbed-wire fence next to the gate, careful not to snag my jeans. It was lucky this wasn't a shorts wearing day, mostly because of my lunch meeting with Dawn. I was already sweating in the Florida sun, and hoped this was the right place. My GPS had directed me to the spot, but it wouldn't be the first time Siri had been wrong. After a ten-minute walk, I saw the cabin, with Mardy Jackson's SUV parked outside. *Bingo.*
I walked onto the porch, papers clutched in my left hand, and knocked.

There was a wait, then a cautious, "Who is it?" through the door.

"Jackson, it's Will Harper. We need to talk."

"Go away. I have nothing to say to you."

"You're going to want to hear what I have to say." It was a bluff, but curiosity is a powerful thing.

The door opened slowly, and Jackson looked out, peering around Will's shoulder to see if anyone was with him. "What do you want?"

"I guess you know that Andy Mays body washed up on the beach."

"Yes, what's that got to do with me?"

"Did you know that Curt Stoneham has disappeared?"

"Shit. Still, why should I care?"

"I know about your deal with Stoneham, he wrote it down before he disappeared."

Jackson's eyes widened, and I held the papers towards him. He took them from me, handling them the way he might a poisonous snake. Without reading them, he said "He's lying. We never had any deal."

"Oops. My mistake. You've been served." I turned to walk away, leaving him standing open-mouthed at the door. As I stepped off the porch, I added a warning. "Listen, Mardy, it didn't take me long to find you, and I'll bet whoever else you're hiding from won't be far behind. You might want to think about leaving town until the trial on that lawsuit." It was good advice, but I gave it too late. The Wolf was nearly at the door.

§

Actually, Bo Wolf was still waiting behind the barn when he saw Will Harper walk back up the gravel drive, step gingerly over the barbed-wire fence, get in his car, and drive back towards town. He let a few minutes go by, got out of the truck and made his way over to the gate. Time to see who was at the end of that driveway.

Chapter Twenty-Five

It was past 6:30 when I got back to Sandy's marina, and I hoped that dinner and our evening together hadn't gone up in smoke. The lights were on in her sailboat, and I knocked on the hull before boarding. "Permission to come aboard?" I held my breath for her answer.

"Who could that be? It can't be my date; he was supposed to be here *hours* ago." She stuck her head out of the hatch, and I was relieved to see a smile. "Hello, Will, come here and kiss me."

I complied, and said, "Sorry I'm so late, but it was for a good cause."

"You're here now, and that's what matters. Can I pour you a glass of wine? I'm a glass ahead of you already." She poured the chilled Chardonnay, handed it to me, and we sat in the cockpit of her boat watching the sun sink lower in the sky. "Now tell me about your day, *mon cheri*."

And so I did, starting with hiding Dawn, shipping her documents to Walter, the setting up of her deposition, and taking her out to lunch. I confess I soft peddled the last part a little, not wanting to rock the boat. At least not yet. She was pleased by my efforts to find Mardy Jackson and serve the filing of the suit against him, and she couldn't resist teasing me when I described climbing over the barbed-wire fence.

"Will, please tell me you did not get cut on that rusty wire?"

"Nope, made it over unscathed."

"Perhaps I should get a flashlight and inspect for myself."

I put an arm around her. "After dinner you can inspect all you want. No bright lights necessary."

She leaned into me. "Seriously though, do you think this lawsuit against Jackson will do any good?"

"It's already doing one thing, and that is it's making a lot of people around the River Walk project very nervous. The more worried they are, the more likely they are to make a mistake. Mardy Jackson hiding out is a good example of that."

We sat in silence for a moment, then she spoke. "Tell me about this Dawn. Is she pretty?"

Uh oh. "You know, just kind of average looking, why?"

"You are taking her to lunch, going to her hotel room, I just thought I should know what she looks like, that's all."

It was time to change the direction of this conversation. "Do you know what she showed me?

Her eyebrows arched as she looked at me. "What?"

"She showed me drawings that Andy Mays did of the

marina, diner and bait shack the way he envisioned them looking in the River Walk. He drew them with tin roofs and porches, bright colors and palm trees, in an old Florida style that would work perfectly with the new buildings next to them."

"Will, that sounds wonderful! Why did they want to tear down our businesses then?"

"Because it's not what Dolphin River Partners wanted. They want upscale chain restaurants and shops, not a place to hang out and drink a beer, or fish on the water. Andy saw what it could be, but they shut him down."

It was a grim reminder of finding his body a few feet from where we sat. I wished I hadn't said it.

"We must not let them win," she said. "We owe that to Andy and his family." She hugged me tightly, and added, "Tonight we will celebrate being alive."

I picked up my wine. "I'll drink to that."

§

When Bo Wolf moved closer to the cabin at the end of the driveway, he crept into the brush along the edge, not wanting to be seen until he knew who was there. As he edged near, he spotted Mardy Jackson's SUV. *Well, look who we have here.* He was practically licking his lips in anticipation of this encounter. Jackson was carrying his bags out to the car, apparently ready to leave, but it was too late for that. As he tossed his bags in the back and closed the hatch, he saw Wolf's reflection in the glass.

"Hey there, Mardy. You've been avoiding me, haven't you?"

Jackson spun around, saw the gun in Wolf's hand, and put

his hands in the air. "Listen, Bo, it's not like that at all. I've been staying out of sight because of the lawsuit that damn reporter filed. He was just here, serving me papers."

The gun never wavered. "Mr. Harper was kind enough to lead me straight to you, Mardy. It's a good thing, because I was getting real tired of driving around looking for you." He motioned towards the house with the gun. "Anyone else here with you?"

"No, I'm alone."

"Well, let's go in and have a little chat. If there's any surprises inside, remember that this gun is pointed at your back. It wouldn't be a good idea to startle me."

Keeping his hands up, Jackson walked into the house. The cabin was only two rooms and a bath, and Wolf soon confirmed that they were alone.

"Have a seat in that chair, Mardy. You're looking a little shaky there."

Jackson sat down and wiped his brow with his sleeve. "What do you want, Bo?"

"Guess you heard that Mays fellow washed up on the beach. I figure the cops are going to want to talk to me about that sooner or later and I'd just as soon avoid that. You remember that raise I talked to you about?"

"Listen, our working arrangement is over. I never asked you to kill Andy Mays, you did that on your own. Leave me out of this."

"Why Mardy, I'm surprised at you. The only reason I was anywhere near Mays was because you were afraid he was going to blow the whistle on your little deal with Curt Stoneham, buying houses near the River Walk before anyone else knew about it." The look in his eyes belied his genial tone. "Leaving you out just isn't going to happen."

"That was all Curt's idea, not mine. He got the money from Dolphin River Partners, not me. I won't make anything until I develop those properties and that might be years. You need to get the money you want from him, mine's all tied up in real estate."

"I'm real sorry to hear that, Mardy. You see, Curt had a little accident, kind of like what happened to Andy Mays." His eyes narrowed. "The same sort of accident you're about to have."

As soon as he heard the words, Jackson flew out of the chair at Wolf, turning sideways to make himself a smaller target. The gun went off next to his head as he crashed into Bo's chest, taking them both to the floor. His ears were ringing from the gun shot as Jackson wrestled Wolf for the gun, and he could feel that he was beginning to lose the battle. Wolf outweighed him by fifty pounds and a lot of muscle, and Jackson's surprise attack was the only reason he wasn't already dead. The two men struggled for control of the gun, and when the muzzle began to turn slowly as Wolf's hand overpowered Jackson's grip, Mardy did the only thing he could think of. He sank his teeth into Bo Wolf's hand.

Howling in pain, Wolf dropped the gun from his bleeding hand, leaped up and aimed a kick at Jackson's head, ready to end this and inflict some pain of his own. He never got the chance. Mardy grabbed the gun from the floor and shot Bo Wolf.

Bright red blood blossomed on his chest as he looked at Jackson in disbelief. He opened his mouth to speak, but only red bubbles passed his lips. His eyes glazed over and he fell backwards onto the rug, dead.

Mardy Jackson lay back on the floor, exhausted, ears ringing, nausea over what he'd done mixed with relief to still be alive. When he felt like he could breathe again, he got up and looked at the body. Wolf's vacant eyes stared at the ceiling, a surprised look on his face. He hadn't expected to be the one to lose.

I've got to get out of here, was Jackson's first thought. His bags were already in his car, and he searched Wolf's pockets for the cash he had on him. Just a few hundred. *That can't be all the money he has*. Jackson went outside and searched Bo's truck, finding his bag of clothes and toiletries, but no more money. It was obvious that Wolf was leaving town, and Mardy knew he wouldn't go empty handed. He searched under the seats, the glove compartment, and in the toolbox in the back, finding nothing.

Puzzled, he opened the tailgate, got down to the level of the truck bed and peered under it where the raised rails kept it from being flush with the bed. It was too dark in the small crevice to see anything, so he retrieved a flashlight from his car and shined it under the gap. Looking closely, he could see that the base of the toolbox extended into the truck's bed on the left side. He opened the lid, and looked at the flat bottom. Nothing obvious. *Hmmmmm*. On the inside corner where the bottom of the box connected he saw a small scratch. Pushing against it, nothing moved.

Jackson returned to the cabin, gave Bo Wolf's cooling body a wide berth, and pulled an old-style can and bottle opener from the kitchen drawer. He went out to the truck, leaned in the toolbox, and slipped the point of the opener into the spot where the scratch was. Wiggling the point in, he was able to lift the bottom enough to get a finger under it. The sharp metal sliced his skin, and he yelped and dropped it flat. *Shit*. It was a deep cut, and he returned to the cabin, holding his hand up as the blood dripped from his finger. Going into the bathroom he located the first aid kit and cleaned and bandaged his finger.

He walked around the body and went back to his effort to get into the compartment he now believed to be under the toolbox. He took a shirt from Bo's duffle and wrapped it around his injured hand, used the bottle opener to pry open the bottom of the toolbox once more, and shoved his padded hand under the metal before it could drop back down. He got a good grip this time, and lifted the false bottom out. *Bingo*. Stacks of cash in plastic wrap were wedged into the small space. It wasn't anything near what he'd planned on making on land development, but it might get him a start in Central America.

Mardy Jackson was leaving town.

Chapter Twenty-Six

The evening had been wonderful, and the morning was starting out just fine. Sandy and I were drinking coffee in the salon of her boat, comfortable in spite of the low ceilings. I preferred the wide open spaces of my Grand Banks, but she was a die-hard sailor, and cramped interior spaces were part of the deal. Sailors call power boaters "stink potters" with derision because of our reliance on diesel fuel to get from place to place, usually going on at length about the purity of wind power. The truth is, sailboats nearly all have utility engines to get them in and out of harbors and anchorages, and the vast majority of them are diesel. Go figure.

We hadn't wanted to spoil the mood last night with a lot of conversation about the eminent domain battle or the lawsuit against Mardy Jackson, so I brought her up to speed this morning. She was particularly amused that I had tracked Jackson to his cabin in the middle of nowhere.

"Did he wet his pants when you showed up at the door, Will?"

I laughed, and said, "Not exactly, but he was surprised I'd found him so easily. I got the feeling he'd be clearing out of there as soon as I left."

"Is that going to be a problem, if we are suing him and he

is not here?"

"I doubt that he'll be out of touch with his lawyers; but now that he's been served, he can't claim to be unaware of the suit anyway. It can proceed without him if necessary."

Sandy sighed. "This whole thing feels like it's going in circles. They threaten us, we threaten them back, and nothing happens. When will it finally end?"

"If I can keep Dawn DeLuca out of the spotlight long enough to get her to testify, then I think there might still be a chance to stop the eminent domain. She knows enough about the collusion between the city and Dolphin River Partners that the judge could rule against them. Anyway, it's our best shot."

"I'm tired of fighting this, Will. I wish it would be over."

Placing a kiss on her forehead, I said, "Be careful what you wish for."

Later I'd remember that comment.

§

Mardy Jackson was getting desperate. After leaving the cabin and Bo Wolf's body behind, he'd driven to a motel on I-75 where he'd spent the night. His plan when he'd headed to the country was to hide there until things cooled down, not to disappear forever. He'd taken a few clothes and some cash, but his passport and the pass codes for his overseas accounts were still in his office safe. He'd counted the money he'd taken from Bo Wolf's truck and it came to a little more than $28,000, enough to flee, but not enough to start a new life.

In the dingy motel room, he'd come up with a new plan. It meant running the risk of a brief return to Dolphin River to get his papers, but it came with an added benefit; a free ride to Cancun, Mexico.

When morning came, Jackson put his bags in the car and drove back towards Dolphin River. With the cabin's remote location he didn't think the body would be discovered for days, so no one would be looking for him. When he got to his office he parked across the street and waited in the car to see if anyone was watching. After a half an hour, nothing looked out of place, so he exited the car and walked to his office door, slipped the key in the lock, and entered. He locked the front door and went into the inner office.

He shut the door so that anyone looking through the glass from the sidewalk would think the business was closed, and turned on the light. *So far, so good.* The safe was in the corner, and he knelt in front of it, punched in the combination and pulled open the heavy door.

He retrieved his passport, the list of account codes and the cash he kept on hand for emergencies, then closed the safe. He went to the closet and took a first aid kit off the shelf. Jackson didn't want to stay in the office any longer than necessary, but his finger was throbbing from where he sliced it on Bo's truck. He cleaned the injury, bandaged it and was back out of the building with the door locked behind him in minutes. He looked both ways, crossed the street to his car, and drove off with a sigh of relief.

Step one complete. Now for the hard part. He'd have to stay out of sight until it was nearly dark, and then drive to the Dolphin River Marina. He had a boat to catch.

§

It had been a frustrating day. I'd called Dawn DeLuca with the details on the deposition and told her Walter had arranged to have a junior attorney pick her up and take her to the rented office space where she could get her story on the record. The only problem was that she was getting cold feet.

"Will, I want to help, but I'm scared. What if they come after me next?"

"I've tried to tell you, Dawn, the best way to insure your safety is to get your testimony on the record. There's no reason to harm you if the damage to their case is already done."

"But you said I'd need to testify, that the deposition wouldn't be enough by itself."

"That's true, but we'll keep you out of sight until then." There was silence on the phone. "Dawn, are you still there?"

"I'm not sure I should do this."

"As long as you have the knowledge of the city's wrongdoing and don't make it public, you're at risk." I was tired of repeating myself.

"All right, I'll do the deposition, but I'm not promising I'll testify. I need to think about it."

This was giving me a headache. "Do you need me to go with you to the deposition?"

"Oh Will, that would be wonderful. I'd feel much better with you there."

I'd been trying to keep my distance from her, both to avoid her obvious attraction to me, and to stay out of trouble with Sandy, but hell, this was all about helping Sandy, after all. "OK,

I'll call Walter and tell him that I'll bring you myself. No point in having his staff make an unnecessary trip."

We hung up, and I called our attorney to let him know about the change in plans. I thought I heard a touch of amusement in his voice.

"Miss DeLuca isn't getting hung up on her knight in shining armor is she, Will?"

"Nothing like that. She just needs a little hand-holding." As soon as I said it, I knew it was a poor choice of words. "Uh, I mean, she wants me to walk her through the process, because I'm the one she knows. Not some stranger, right?"

Walter chuckled. "You don't have to convince me. I'm guessing Sandy is the one you'll have to convince that this is just about being helpful."

That was something I didn't need right now; a jealous girlfriend. Resigned to my fate, I wrapped up the writing projects I was in the middle of, and finished just in time to go pick up Dawn. On the drive to the motel on Bradenton Beach the thought crossed my mind that I'd better mention 'my girlfriend Sandy' at some point during my time with my clingy witness. Hopefully, she'd get the point.

The situation was one that frustrated me. I wasn't attracted to Dawn, she was attracted to me. Since I wasn't available, being committed to my relationship with Sandy, why was this my problem? It was a conversation I'd had once with my ex-wife, and it hadn't gone well. A woman I worked with at the newspaper had developed a crush on me, and I thought the easiest way to deal with it was to ignore it. Not my ex.

She'd said, "Will, you're being blind. If she puts the moves on you, you'll fold like cardboard."

"Hey, that's not fair. I have no intention of cheating on you, whether she wants me to or not! You act like I have no choice in the matter."

"You're a man, you can't resist a woman who wants you."

I was hoping Sandy didn't have the same low opinion of me.

When I arrived at the motel I knocked and Dawn came to the door. "Hi Will, come on in, I'll be ready to go in a minute." I stepped into the dim motel room, but stayed near the door as she checked her face in the bathroom mirror. She touched up her lipstick and picked up her purse. "Now I'm ready to face this, let's go."

We walked out to my car and I held the door as she got in the passenger side. The low-slung car isn't easy to get into, and she held her hand out to me for support as she wedged herself into the small seat. All I could think of was the 'hand-holding' comment I'd made without thinking. *Crap, I don't need this today.* We drove to the rented space where the deposition was to take place, and I walked her inside and turned her over to Gary Adams, a junior attorney in Walter Lord's firm. He'd be conducting the deposition with Walter listening in by phone.

"Will, won't you stay here with me?" Dawn asked.

"Sorry, but I'm sure Walter and Gary don't want me getting in the way. I'd better run a few errands and come back when it's nearer time for you to be finished."

Gary chimed in, "Actually, it's no problem if you want to

sit in, Will." My dirty look didn't register with him.

"That's great, you'll stay won't you Will?"

Groan. "Sure, why not?"

§

It was late afternoon when I was finally able to drop Dawn DeLuca back at the motel and make my escape. She'd practically pleaded with me to take her to dinner or at least have a drink with her. When I told her I wished I could but that I had plans with my girlfriend Sandy, she looked at me like I'd just told her that her dog had died. Disappointing her didn't feel good, but I was breathing a sigh of relief that I had done the right thing and defused the situation. I drove back to my boat at SailFin Point Marina, only feeling a little guilty that I had lied to Dawn about having plans already. It was, after all, for a good cause.

I was walking down the ramp to my boat when I saw Captain Rick running towards me, his footsteps making a staccato beat on the wooden pier.

"Will, where the hell have you been, I've been calling you for two hours!"

"Damn, I'm sorry, Rick, I turned my ringer off while I was in the deposition, what's up?"

He stopped to catch his breath, then told me. "I was coming back from crabbing two hours ago, running my little skiff up the Manatee River when I saw it."

"Saw what, Rick?"

"I saw that sailboat of Sandy's motoring out towards the bay, and she wasn't at the wheel. Some man was."

"What did he look like?" My first fearful thought was Bo Wolf.

"Just a regular guy, kind of thin, brown hair. He didn't look much like he knew how to pilot a boat though, seemed nervous. I tried to catch up and ask him what he was doing on Sandy's boat, but the damn spark-plug on that crappy old Johnson picked right then to foul out. By the time I got it started again, they were out of sight."

"They? I thought you said he was driving."

"Before the boat got to the bay, I saw a woman with long hair join him in the cockpit. I think it was Sandy."

Chapter Twenty-Seven

Sandy St. Martin was tired after a long day. The marina was a never-ending series of projects that needed to be done, and she'd made a dent in a few of them. A quick shower, a glass or two of wine, and she was going to bed. She'd turned on the hot water, stripped, and was about to get in when she felt the boat move as if someone had stepped aboard.

What the hell? Will knew better than to drop by unannounced. She turned off the water, grabbed a beach coverup and slipped it on. She grabbed an empty wine bottle by the neck, and approached the steps to the hatchway. Before she could reach it, the hatch opened, and Mardy Jackson stepped down into the cabin holding a gun aimed at her.

"Miss St. Martin, my gun trumps your wine bottle. Why don't you put it down."

"What do you want?"

"We're going for a little ride."

§

Jackson found some smaller dock lines in the cabin and tied her hands and feet, then tied her to the main mast where it passed through the cabin to its base in the keel. He wasn't about to have her go after him with a bottle, or anything else. He needed her to sail the boat. He had never sailed, but he grew up close enough to the water that he'd spent a little time running his friend's small boats. He figured he could untie the lines and motor out into the bay before the sun set. Then he'd cut her loose, make her put up the sails and head for Mexico. Cancun was only 540 miles across the Gulf and they wouldn't have to worry about running out of fuel.

Jackson looked outside the cabin, saw no one nearby on the dock and went out to cast off the lines. Just before he pulled the last one free, he remembered to start the auxiliary engine. *I have to pay attention if I'm going to get out of here*, he thought. He looked next to the oversized wheel for the ignition switch and saw that it needed a key. He stepped back into the cabin and walked over to where Sandy was trussed to the mast. "Where's the key?"

"Go to hell."

He slapped her viciously, and a trickle of blood ran from her lip. "Where's the key?"

She knew she needed to survive until she could find a chance to fight back. "It's hanging on a hook inside the food locker next to the stove."

Jackson retrieved the key, returned to the cockpit, made

sure the ignition was in neutral and started the engine. The exhaust bubbled quietly through the water as he tossed the last line onto the dock and slowly backed out, slightly bumping the dock as he did. Turning the bow towards the river, he motored into the channel, careful to maintain a slow speed in the No Wake zone. The last thing he wanted right now was to attract attention.

The Au Revoir passed the shacks and homes of the Dolphin River waterfront and soon entered the wider channel of the Manatee River. *So far, so good.* It would take more than an hour with the slow pace of the sailboat under power to reach the open water of the Gulf, and Mardy considered his options. Boat traffic was light this time of day, but the last thing he needed was for Sandy to signal a passing vessel that she was in trouble. He decided to leave her tied up below and handle the boat himself for as long as he could.

A few boats passed by, making their way home after a day on the water, and he gave them a friendly wave, hoping no one would recognize either him or the boat. One old guy in a skiff looked at him oddly as he passed by. He wondered if the man knew something was wrong, but he seemed to be having problems with his motor and the skiff drifted away while Jackson drove the Au Revoir out of the river into the mouth of Tampa Bay. He smiled and thought, *I just might get away with this.* It was time to bring Sandy St. Martin to the cockpit.

He looked to see that there was no boat traffic nearby, then throttled the engine to idle and went below to untie her.

"You look like you're ready for some fresh air. We're going up on deck."

Her eyes flashed anger at him; blood had dried on her lips where he'd struck her. "Why should I help you with anything?"

"Because if you don't, I'll toss you overboard. It's a long way to swim with your hands tied." He saw fear cross her face. "Look, I didn't bring you along because I want to kill you, although I should for how you've screwed up my plans. You and your reporter boyfriend ruined a good thing, so now it's your turn to help me get out of here."

"How do you think you're going to run away in a sailboat? You've been running the engine for more than an hour. There's not enough fuel to get anywhere."

He grinned and said, "That's where you come in. We're sailing this boat to Cancun."

"You're out of your mind! We don't have provisions or charts to go that far."

"Oh, but that's where you're wrong. I read those articles about your marina in the paper and they said you sailed this boat singlehandedly from the Virgin Islands to Florida. I know you are capable, so don't lie to me."

"Listen, I made that trip after lots of planning, and made quite a few stops along the way. You're talking about sailing across a body of water I know nothing about, with no place to stop and re-provision. It's too dangerous to try it."

"I wasn't asking for your opinion, I'm telling you what we're doing. Now, are you going to go put those sails up?"

Sandy decided her best bet was to cooperate. She could count on Will to come after her, and the distinctive red and blue chevron on her main sail would be easy to spot from the air.

"*Oui.* Untie me."

He held his gun on her as he cut the lines binding her to the mast, then cut her wrists loose. She rubbed them together to get the circulation going, and he prodded her with the muzzle. "Get up there."

"Can I at least put some pants on?"

"You won't be needing them." Jackson had noticed her lack of underwear when he'd been tying her to the mast, and while he had more important things to deal with, it might provide a little diversion once they were a long way from shore.

When they made their way on deck, Sandy saw the boat was rocking in the waves. "I need to get us underway before I put the sail up. The deck is pitching too much."

"Do it."

She put the boat back in gear, pushed the throttle forward and locked the wheel in place. Sandy then stepped lightly to the main mast, pulled the cover and the ties off of the sail, ran the sheet through the winch and hoisted it aloft. The sail filled, she returned to the cockpit and killed the engine, and they were underway. As the Au Revoir picked up speed Sandy felt like she could breathe again. With the dying sun on her face and the wind in her hair, she could almost forget why she was here. The feeling didn't last long.

"Why did you only put up one sail, aren't there two? We need all the speed this thing can manage."

"The channel through Tampa Bay isn't wide enough for that to be safe. If we run aground, we won't be going anywhere. We can hoist the jib when we reach open water." She wasn't going to point out that there were actually three sails if you included the spinnaker. No way was she going to fly that sail with a gun at her back. She didn't want to reach open water any sooner than she had to. They'd be a lot harder to find once they entered the Gulf of Mexico.

§

"Listen, Will, if you don't slow down a little when we pass other boats, the Coast Guard is liable to get a report and stop us."

"Good, maybe they'll get a helicopter in the air then." Captain Rick had joined me aboard the WanderLust and we'd headed quickly out into the Manatee River, giving chase to Mardy Jackson. The twin V8 Detroit Diesels on my big Grand Banks are capable of pushing her at fourteen knots, fifteen at nearly the red line, and the sailboat would be going closer to half of that speed. We needed to catch up with Sandy's boat, Au Revoir, before she hit open water. There were simply too many routes they could take. I'd already called the Coast Guard and reported the suspected kidnapping, but they were reluctant to give chase without more to go on. We were on our own.

It was a shot in the dark, but I picked up the microphone on the VHS and turned it to channel 16, the open contact channel. "Notice to all boats in the Tampa Bay area, I'm looking for a stolen sailboat, a Beneteau First 40 model with a large red and blue chevron on the mainsail. Please respond to the boat WanderLust on this channel if you spot it. Thank you."

Rick manned the binoculars, checking out any sails within range of us, but we'd had no luck so far. We were half way through Tampa Bay without sighting them, and I was worried. Once we were past Anna Maria Island into the Gulf and deep water, there was no way to predict their path. Another twenty minutes and we'd have to make a decision.

The time and distance seemed to crawl by, until finally I saw the island in the distance off to port. The Passage Key Inlet hugged the shore and was narrower, and the deeper Egmont Key shipping channel was several miles to starboard. Which one would they have taken? If Jackson was trying to run to Key West or the Bahamas, Passage Key would be the most direct route. Even though it's narrow, it's deep enough for a sailboat the size of Sandy's. If he was going for Mexico, the bigger channel at Egmont Key would make sense. I decided to go for Passage Key.

I was less than a mile from the channel when I heard the radio. "WanderLust, WanderLust, this is the freighter China Girl calling. WanderLust, WanderLust."

"Go ahead China Girl, this is WanderLust."

"Hey WanderLust, I believe we sighted that stolen boat you sent out a bulletin on. White hull, main sail has a blue and white chevron on it."

"Where are you located, China Girl?"

"Just passed through the Egmont Key ship channel and the boat is about a half mile ahead of us. We might not have noticed it, but the stupid fool behind the wheel cut it close coming across our bow to get into the channel ahead of us. He must not know it takes us damn near half a mile to turn this ship."

"Could you tell which way he's heading, China Girl?"

"His heading was SouthWest, roughly 230 degrees. Good

luck catching him."

"Thanks for the assist, China Girl. WanderLust out."

"Rick, can you chart me a course to go out the Egmont Key channel, then intercept them on a heading of 230 in the Gulf?"

"You got it, Will."

Now at least we had a chance.

Chapter Twenty-Eight

Mardy Jackson was starting to feel better. Sandy St. Martin had scared the crap out of him when she'd run the boat across the path of that big freighter, and they'd bounced heavily through the wake as it passed them. He'd then threatened to tie her back up, but she knew he needed her. Once through the channel he'd made her lash the wheel in place and held his gun on her as she raised the jib, adding some much needed speed to the boat. He'd brought along a basic chart of the Gulf that he'd printed off the internet, so he'd know if she tried to go the wrong way.

Watching the wind pluck at her beach cover-up was both distracting and entertaining, a sure sign that he was feeling better. *Hmm, I'd like to see what she looks like without it*, he thought. He grinned at the confirmation that French women like to keep their body hair natural, unlike many American women these days. Things were definitely looking up.

§

More than forty-five minutes had passed since the sighting from the freighter. We should have spotted them by now. I was getting worried that the move in front of the ship had been a feint. Get their attention, take off on a clear heading, then change directions once they were over the horizon. It's what I would have done, but I was betting that Jackson didn't know enough about boats to think of that.

Captain Rick had bleary eyes from staring into the binoculars in the fading light, and I was about to offer to trade places when he grabbed my arm. "Will! I think it's them." He handed me the high powered Nikons and pointed.

"Where, Rick, I don't see them."

"Look right at the horizon line, just off the right corner of the bow pulpit."

I strained to see in the dim light. There was a flash of white sail in the sunset. "It's them. Let's go." I retook the wheel and pushed the throttles to the stops. The hull shuddered as it fought against the waves, powering to the tops and then smashing down into the troughs. It was a rough ride and I hoped I wasn't causing any leaks, but there was no choice. We had to catch them while there was still light. It was a painful ten minutes as the sun sank lower, but we were finally close enough for them to spot us. Through the binoculars I saw Jackson standing in front of the wheel, Sandy sitting behind it in the pilot's seat. He had a gun aimed at her.

"Rick, take the wheel. Get us as close as you can, and I'm going to jump aboard from the bow pulpit."

"You're crazy! He'll shoot you before you can jump."

"I'm going to lay down on the bow. This boat is so much taller than the sailboat's deck that he won't have an angle."

"What if he just shoots Sandy instead?"

"It's a gamble, but he needs her to sail to Mexico. There's no way he can do it alone."

Rick put a hand on my arm. "What if you're wrong?"

I took a deep breath. "It's a chance we have to take. He'll kill her for sure once he gets there. If he didn't, she'd turn him in to the Mexican authorities."

He looked grim. "Just tell me what to do."

"Get in close. The way the boats are pitching we'll probably hit. When the pulpit is over their stern, blow the horn. I'll jump up and over onto the deck."

He shook his head. "It's your funeral."

I made my way down to the front of the WanderLust, holding onto the rails as I crouched beneath the sides, then lay down and crawled my way to the pulpit, the protruding platform hanging over the bow. It was handy for retrieving anchors, but today it was being used for something new. I heard Jackson yell threats at me, and when I peeked over the pitching deck I could see him point the gun as we drew near. I put my head down as a shot flew overhead, but the likelihood of him hitting me with a pistol from one pitching boat to another was small. At least, that's what I kept telling myself.

Finally, the sails were so close they seemed to tower above the WanderLust, and I was surprised we hadn't collided yet. Two shots thudded into the hull below me. Then we hit.

The WanderLust's horn thundered above my head, and I rose up and leaped onto the deck of the sailboat. I crashed right into Jackson, sending both of us tumbling and the gun flying. He was on his feet quickly, and came at me snarling, fighting like a tiger. I rolled away and climbed to my feet as he flew at me again, and I caught a quick glance at Sandy, who had her feet tied to the wheel post. Then I saw stars as he crashed a fist into the side of my head.

Shaking my head to clear it, I heard Sandy scream, "Look out!"

I rolled to my right as Jackson swung a winch handle at me, and I heard it whistle past my head.

I had rolled into a corner with nowhere to go without standing, and he stood over me and held the winch handle like a club. "You idiot reporter! Why didn't you stay out of my business."

"You made it my business, asshole, when you sent Bo Wolf to threaten us and those people in the trailer park."

Jackson grinned. "Bo Wolf is dead, and you're about to join him." He lifted the winch handle high to crash it down on my head. I raised my hands to ward off the blow, then felt the deck roll as Sandy threw the Au Revoir into a sudden jibe. The boom of the mast flew from one side to the other with the shift in the wind, struck Mardy Jackson in the head and pitched him into the water.

I struggled to my feet and made my way to Sandy. "Are you all right?"

"Yes, just untie me." She stood as I undid the knots, threw

her arms around me and squeezed until I could scarcely breathe. "Thank God you're all right. She released me, then turned and stared at the spot where Jackson had gone over the rail. "Is he dead?"

"Probably. If it wasn't for you I'd be the one floating out there instead."

She shuddered and walked to the rail. "Should we look for him?'

"It's almost dark. Not much chance we'll spot him."

Captain Rick had been idling nearby with the WanderLust, following the battle with my binoculars, and he pulled alongside and leaned over the railing from the bridge. "Everyone OK over there?" he yelled.

"Jackson went overboard when the boom hit him."

"I saw it. Good riddance, I say."

"We thought about looking for him, but it's almost dark."

"Don't bother. I put the binoculars on him when he went in, and he was floating face down and trailing blood." I could see the grin light up his face. "The fins circled him in two minutes. Sunset is feeding time for the bull sharks around here."

Mardy Jackson seemed unlikely to show up the way Andy Mays had. There wouldn't be enough left to float.

§

Talking between two pitching boats on the ocean wasn't easy and we didn't want to use the radio, but Rick agreed to take my boat back to the marina while I helped Sandy sail the Au Revoir back to her dock. I don't usually let anyone else pilot the WanderLust without me, but this was different, and Rick was an accomplished captain. Hell, he knew more about boats and piloting than I did by a long shot. He promised not to talk to anyone about what he'd seen and I told him I'd explain it all back at the dock. You can't beat a friend who will do a thing like that for you.

He turned the WanderLust towards land, hit the throttles and was soon out of sight. Sandy turned her boat into the wind, and we sailed slowly along the same path. While she held the wheel I retrieved the gun from the scupper on the port side. That's where it slid when I jumped onto the boat and crashed into Jackson. After a moment's hesitation, I heaved it overboard. I wasn't sure we were free of the need for protection, but Jackson had said Bo Wolf was dead, and that meant it was very possible that he'd used the gun to kill him. I sure didn't need to carry a murder weapon around with me.

Truthfully, I wasn't a fan of guns. It seemed that too often they get turned against their owners, and I felt safer without one. I asked Sandy where to find a cleaning cloth, and she directed me to a deck locker. I took the cloth, dipped it in the water, and wiped the spot off of the boom where it had struck Mardy Jackson in the head. I located a powerful flashlight and looked around for any other signs of the fight that had killed him, but didn't spot any. Hosing down the deck when we docked the boat would be a good idea.

Sitting down next to Sandy at the helm, I put an arm around her. "Are you OK?"

"*Oui.*" The look on her face said otherwise.

"Want to talk about it?"

"Oh, Will, I always loved this boat. Now two men have died aboard her, and I killed one of them."

There wasn't a lot I could say about that. "You had no choice. Jackson would have killed us both."

"But I have been so many miles on Au Revoir, and she was my home. Now all I can think of is the bodies, the blood, the death." Tears ran down her cheeks as she spoke.

There wasn't any more comfort I could offer, so I just held her.

It was very late when we returned to her slip at the Dolphin River Marina, tied it to the dock and hosed it down. Rinsing off the salt spray before it dries is standard procedure with boaters, so we didn't attract any undue attention with the late night wash down. Finally, we were done.

I took her in my arms. "Would you like to come to my boat tonight?"

"*Oui*. I cannot sleep here." I'd suspected as much.

We packed a bag for her, locked the cabin and walked up the dock to my car. For this night, she would be safe with me.

Chapter Twenty-Nine

When we arrived at the WanderLust, a light was on, and we entered cautiously. It was only Captain Rick, asleep in a chair. I shook him awake. "Rick, we're back."

He sat up, rubbed his eyes, and struggled to alertness. "Thought I'd better know what the story is before morning in case anyone comes around asking."

"Thanks. Let me make some coffee and I'll fill you in."

Sandy said, "I'm going to bed, I don't want to hear this again." She leaned over and gave Rick a hug. "Thank you for coming to my rescue. Will told me that you were the one who spotted my boat leaving. If you hadn't called him and come after me, I'd be gone."

He blushed, and said, "I'm glad you're safe. That's all that matters."

She closed the cabin door as I started the coffee brewing,

then I sat down across from Captain Rick. "I guess you're wondering why we didn't want the authorities involved."

"A little, yes. I mean, there were three of us that witnessed what happened. No one would blame you or Sandy for Jackson's death."

With a sigh, I began to explain. "You're right, but there's something you don't know. Someone murdered Andy Mays on Sandy's boat. It was a setup to make her look guilty."

He looked shocked. "Why didn't you tell me?"

This was hard to admit. "Because we took the boat offshore and dumped the body."

Rick was stunned. "Why would you do that, Will?"

"You have to understand, Andy was killed on her boat, the likely murder weapon was Sandy's and someone had called the police to report a disturbance on the dock. She'd have gone to jail while they sorted it out. And since she called me first and I was there, I might have gone to jail with her. I wanted to tell you, but it would have made you an accomplice. Disposing of the body was a crime."

He looked unhappy. "Guess I'm an accomplice now."

"I'm so sorry that it worked out this way, Rick. If we reported what happened with Mardy Jackson, the police would be all over Sandy's boat with a forensics team. There's no way to be sure we got rid of every trace of Andy's blood, and it would be impossible to explain what we did if they found something. I'm afraid this was the only way."

He was silent for a bit, and I waited to let him think it through. Finally, he spoke. "I guess you're right, even if I don't like it. I appreciate that you were trying to keep me out of it, but now that I'm involved anyway, we have to have an understanding." He gave me a hard look.

"OK."

"From now on, no secrets. If we're going to be friends, tell me the truth, even if it makes you look bad."

"You've got it, Rick."

"Do you think this will be the end of it, or is someone else going to come after Sandy?"

"There's no way to know for sure, but Jackson told me that Bo Wolf was dead. He was the biggest threat, and I don't think any of the people in the mayor's office have the stomach for violence. I hope this is over."

"That makes two of us."

We'd have to wait to find out.

§

I slept in after the late night, and woke when the phone rang at nearly noon. "Hello?"

"Is this Will Harper?"

"Yes?" The official sounding voice made me nervous.

"This is Chief Petty Officer Rob Johnson, U.S. Coast Guard. Did you report a boat missing yesterday?"

"Oh, yes, I'm sorry I didn't call you back. It was my girlfriend's boat and she wasn't answering the radio. She made it back to the dock OK."

"Mister Harper, next time you make a report like that, please keep us posted when there is a change. The Coast Guard doesn't need to waste resources on a wild goose chase."

"My apologies, please. Honestly, it seemed like the Coast Guard wasn't taking it too seriously, so I didn't think I needed to call and cancel anything."

"We take everything seriously, sir. Just let us know next time something like this happens."

"Absolutely, thanks for your concern." I hung up the phone, both relieved and annoyed. I'd tried my damnedest to get them to intervene yesterday with no luck, and today, they wanted me to keep them in the loop. Go figure. Anyway, it was nice to know we weren't forgotten by the Coasties.

Stumbling out of bed after the rude awakening, I smelled coffee from the front cabin. I climbed the short ladder to the salon, and was greeted by the sight of Sandy wearing one of my shirts and nothing else, legs tucked under her in my favorite chair as she drank coffee and read one of my boating magazines.

She welcomed me with a smile. "I wondered how long you would sleep."

"I was pretty worn out from last night."

"So was I. Is everything all right with Captain Rick?"

"Yes, he agreed that we didn't have a lot of choice in what we did. He was kind of pissed that I had lied to him, though. He made me promise not to keep secrets from him in the future."

"Can you really agree to that?"

I grinned, and said "We all have a very good reason to protect each other's secrets. That makes it easier to be open. Rick has been a good friend, and now we know he's a friend we can trust with anything."

Sandy called the marina and told Enrique that she

wouldn't be at work today, so we had the afternoon to ourselves. We spent a lazy day on my boat, took the skiff out for a swim on a nearby island, and were back in the salon drinking margaritas when my phone rang.

"Hello, Will?"

"Hey, Walter, what's up?"

"Have you been listening to the news today?"

"No, to be honest, we've been avoiding it. What's going on?"

"The police found a body at Mardy Jackson's cabin near the Myakka State Park. It's been tentatively identified as Bo Wolf."

I tried to act surprised. "Wow, that is big news. Did they catch Jackson?"

"No, and when they went to Bo Wolf's trailer to follow up, there were signs of a struggle there. The police searched the property and found a shallow grave. Guess who was in it?"

Now I really was in the dark. "Who?"

"Curt Stoneham. He'd been shot in the head."

Damn. That means the gun I tossed overboard had likely killed at least two people. I was glad I hadn't held on to it. I made a mental note to dig the two slugs Mardy Jackson had fired at me out of the WanderLust's bow and toss them into deep water.

"It sounds like the opposition is dropping like flies, Walter."

"Yes, and this should make Dawn DeLuca feel a lot more comfortable about testifying."

I'd nearly forgotten about Dawn with last night's adventure. "Does she know about Curt's death?"

"I called to let her know. She was pretty broken up about it, but relieved that Bo Wolf wouldn't be coming after her."

"Thanks for calling her, I know she appreciated it."

"Just part of my job. It shouldn't be long now until I hear from the judge about my petition to dismiss the eminent domain action based on Dawn's deposition. It makes it pretty obvious that there was improper influence from Dolphin River Partners in the effort to take those businesses, if not outright bribery. Keep your fingers crossed."

"What do you think the odds are?"

"No better than fifty-fifty."

"Even with proof of wrongdoing by both the city and Dolphin River Partners? That doesn't make sense."

"You have to understand the legal system, Will. The judge has already ruled that the eminent domain case is going forward. To stop it he has to reverse himself, and judges hate doing that. It's more likely that he'll increase the amount the city has to pay, but there's no guarantee of that either."

I shook my head. "Sounds like a lousy system to me."

"It's better than most countries. The problem is that any time a case involves the government versus a citizen, the court is *part* of the government. It's like asking a judge to rule against himself. Not an easy task."

Now I was just depressed. "Thanks for calling, Walter. I'll let Sandy know what you said."

"Don't give up. We've got a lot better case than we started with."

I said goodbye and cut off the call. Sandy had been listening, and looked towards me.

"That didn't sound good. What did he say?"

"Walter doesn't think the judge is going to stop the eminent domain action."

"How can he not? *Thees* is so unfair!"

"He says the judge probably won't reverse an order he's already made. He does think the amount the city pays should go up, though."

"Shit. After everything we've been through, all of this *death*, nothing has changed."

"Sandy, that's not true. Walter's working his tail off to get you a better deal, and that's worth a lot. I told you from the start that he said stopping the eminent domain and saving the marina was a long shot."

"I cannot stand this. I am going home to my boat."

Grabbing her arm, I said "Don't run off. We'll deal with this together, like we have from the beginning."

"I know this is not your fault, Will, but I have to be alone right now."

She got up and packed her bag, threw on some clothes and was out the door and walking up the dock before I could think of anything to say to stop her. *I'll never understand women.* All we'd been through together, fighting to save her marina, but now she wanted to be alone. I felt like I'd been kicked in the teeth. I stood in the doorway watching her walk away when I heard Rick's voice from the dock.

"Everything OK, Will? You look like you just lost your best friend."

"It kind of feels that way. Can I offer you a beer?"

Even after the late night, he looked much better than I felt. "Don't mind if I do."

I walked to the galley, got two frosty Red Stripes from the cold plate refrigerator, and we sat in the salon as I handed him a bottle. He took a long pull on his beer, and said "Woman trouble?"

"You could say that. Sandy seems to have held onto the idea of stopping the eminent domain completely, and Walter and I both told her from the start that was a long shot."

"Hard to let go of her dream, I guess."

"It's frustrating, though. We've made a lot of progress, and I believe Walter will be able to get her enough money to get out of debt and have a little left over. It sure beats where things started out, but she acts like it's a total loss."

"Give her time, Will, she'll come around."

"Maybe." I wasn't so sure.

Chapter Thirty

It had been a long few weeks since our rescue of Sandy from Mardy Jackson. She and I had spent a little time together after her rapid exit from my boat that night, but she still seemed depressed over the impending loss of her marina. Sandy and her helper Eduardo were doing the minimum required to keep the place running, but it was obvious she'd given up. One evening on my boat, I tried to talk sense to her.

We were sitting on the flybridge in the dark, drinking wine under the starry sky. "Sandy?"

"Yes, my love?" Most guys would take that as a positive start, but I knew it was only a turn of phrase with her.

"I hate it that you've been so down lately."

"I can't help it. It feels like the gods have conspired against me."

"How can you say that? Sure you were kidnapped, but

you survived. Mardy Jackson didn't. You were framed for a murder you didn't commit, but the frame didn't work and now the police have blamed it on Bo Wolf, who is probably the one who did it anyway. Dawn DeLuca is set to testify next week, and she might not have if Wolf hadn't killed Curt Stoneham. Now Wolf is dead too. So many things have gone your way, and I think the jury will give you a fair price for the marina. You've got to count your blessings."

She sighed, and said "I know I should be grateful, Will." She put a hand on my leg. "You've done so much for me, and you saved my life. I will always love you for it."

Uh oh. I think I hear a 'but' coming. "What does that mean for us?"

"Let's not talk about that now. When this case is over, I'll know if I have a business anymore. If I don't, I may need to find a job to pay my parents back what I owe them."

We lapsed into silence, sipping our wine in the night. Keeping this relationship together might take a miracle in court. I hoped Walter had one up his sleeve.

§

The hardest part of relationships for me was in knowing where I stood. I'd guarded my feelings after getting burned badly in my marriage, and had been hesitant to get involved with anyone again. Meeting Sandy had changed all of that. We'd both taken it slowly in the beginning, but when she took the step to make it physical it became more, at least for me. I can do casual sex as well as the next guy, but when I'm spending nights in bed with a beautiful woman I really connect with, it's a different thing.

There was only one problem. I wasn't sure if she felt the same way. There's nothing worse than being the only one in the relationship who is in love, a painful bit of knowledge I'd learned when I discovered my ex, Julie, only cared about me for my American Express Card. My relationship with Sandy had a different problem. I'd saved her life, I was fighting to save her marina or at least her finances, and I'd even loaned her money to keep the business going, but none of it seemed to be enough.

I've always been something of a rescuer, not a trait I'm particularly proud of. There's just something about a woman in need that gets to me, that makes me want to hold her and tell her it will all be OK. Better than being a wife-beater, but still not the healthiest of approaches to building a long-term relationship.

What I've always wanted in a partner is one who makes me a priority, who will drop everything when I need them. That may sound a little demanding, but hey, I'm willing to give the same dedication back to the relationship. I want it to be the two of us against the world, not against each other. With Sandy, it seemed to be somewhere in between. She wasn't working against me, but she wasn't exactly there for me, either.

There was a part of me that wanted to fight it out, to say "Dammit, our relationship is worth it!" There was another part of me that felt like saying "If this is all it means to you, then the hell with it." No matter how you struggle with your half of the relationship, you still only get half the vote, and therein lies the problem. Sandy started life with a lot of advantages, not the least of which included parents who would loan her money to buy a marina thousands of miles from their home, simply to help her fulfill a dream. She should have felt like the luckiest girl in the world, even if the dream didn't survive.

Instead she felt put upon by God. Wow. Every day that I wake up, I thank God for another day, something none of us are guaranteed. You start out the day in the plus column, right? I'm no starry-eyed Pollyanna. Actually, I think I have a fairly realistic outlook on life. Prepare for tomorrow, but live each day as if it were your last. It could be, you know. From heart attacks to car wrecks, anything can take you out. None of us are assured of a long life. I plan to treasure the time I have, and that includes the time I have with a woman.

The only problem is that I want them to do the same. To treasure their life, their gifts, and while they're at it, me. I've always treated women well, but discovered as early as my high school days that it wasn't considered a plus by every woman. Some of them want a bad boy, a wild partier, someone who will get rough with them occasionally. That's just not me. I like to have fun as much as the next guy, but dinner with someone you care about and a night of sharing hopes and dreams over steaks and drinks is a great evening in my book. OK, OK, I do like for the romance to lead to a hot time between the sheets, but that's a part of sharing too. I give all of myself, and I want my partner to be willing to do the same

Sandy always seemed to be holding a part of herself back. I thought that with all we'd been through together, the fear, blood, death and finally rescue, it should have forged a bond, not created a chasm between us. I could feel her pulling away from me as the court case approached. It felt like the beginning of goodbye.

Chapter Thirty-One

The week started out badly. Judge Malcolm Greenlaw ruled that the eminent domain was valid and empaneled a jury to set the fair market value. The following day, the hearing before the jury got started early. I was in the gallery with Sandy, seated next to Ron and Carol Cox, owners of the diner, and Bob and Julia Johnson, owners of the bait shack. The first witness was the mayor, and Blackie Ferguson was in fine form as the city attorney fed him softball questions.

"Mr. Mayor, how did the city come up with the idea that putting a park and a staircase to the waterfront in the middle of the River Walk development would be a good thing for the citizens?"

"Well, sir, it was Andy Mays, God rest his soul, who first came to me with the suggestion to put that park there. He was a bright young man in our planning office, and he'd convinced his boss, Curt Stoneham, that access to the waterfront would be key to the success of the project. Success for the city, that is."

"And were you convinced by his argument?"

"Not at first, no. I'm always hesitant to take property from citizens, even when it's for a valid public use. I asked him why we couldn't just let people get to the riverfront through the marina."

"And what was his response?"

"Andy said that we'd be relying on the marina owner to properly maintain the docks, add handicap access, better lighting, things like that. He felt that only the city could do that. The facility has gotten a little run down, after all."

"So you went with his plan?"

"Yes sir, that's what we did. We made a fair offer to those folks to buy their property for a legitimate public use, and they turned us down flat."

"Mr. Mayor, that's why we're here today, to see if the jury agrees with you. No further questions."

The judge said "Your witness, Mr. Lord."

Walter got up and approached the witness box. "Mayor Ferguson, you've testified that the idea for the park and staircase came from Andy Mays, correct?"

"Yes, that's right."

"It's pretty convenient that Mr. Mays and the other person who could have verified your story, his boss, Curt Stoneham, are both deceased, isn't that true?"

"Well, it's true that they have both passed on, but not that it's in any way convenient for the city of Dolphin River. They were valued employees."

"Isn't it true, Mr. Mayor, that Andy Mays actually lobbied for the marina, diner and the bait shack to be incorporated into the River Walk project? To offer those three businesses modest funds to put new facades on them to give an 'old Florida' look to them? A plan which, incidentally, would cost a fraction of the amount that buying the businesses and tearing them down will cost?"

"Not that I was aware of, no." A drop of sweat ran down his forehead into his eye, and he wiped at it as the salt stung him.

"Wasn't it, in fact, Dolphin River Partners who suggested the park and staircase, and didn't they lobby aggressively for the city to pay for it?"

"No sir, that's not what happened. Once we came up with the park idea, of course they wanted input on how it would best fit in with their project, but the idea came from Andy Mays, like I said."

"No further questions, your honor."

The rest of the afternoon was a long, boring string of appraisers talking about what a depressed area the river front had been prior to the River Walk being announced, and defending the low offers the city made. They showed photographs of the three businesses at their worst, and I had to admit they looked dilapidated. The photos were of the bait shop sign hanging loose on one side, the peeling paint on the marina office and the worn and dirty rear entrance to the diner, with overflowing trash cans lined up in a row. It was pretty grim next to the drawing of the elaborate park surrounding the staircase the city wanted to build to replace them.

When the city attorney rested his case at 4:30, The judge adjourned for the day and instructed Walter to be ready to present the rebuttal first thing the next morning. The six of us left the building and headed to the coffee shop across the street. We sat down at a long table, and a few minutes later Walter joined us, setting his briefcase on the floor.

"That was pretty depressing," I said, a sentiment quickly echoed by he rest of the group.

"I know it seems that way, but the jury hasn't heard our side, yet. Dawn is going to blow them away."

"Don't they have her on a witness list?"

"No, I'm going to present her as a city employee who was reluctant to come forward out of fear for her job and her life."

"Think the judge will go for it?"

"Since Andy Mays and Curt Stoneham were both murdered over this thing, I don't see how he can't. Keep your fingers crossed."

We spent a few more minutes discussing strategy with Walter, then paid the check and went our separate ways. Sandy had ridden with me, and I took her back to the marina.

"Do you want to spend the evening together?"

"No, Will, I'm sorry. I feel like being alone in my 'shabby' marina tonight." The bitterness in her tone was hard to miss, but I was too tired to argue.

"OK, shall I pick you up at 7:30 in the morning for court?"

"*Oui, merci'.*" She leaned over and kissed me on the

cheek before exiting the car and walking down the dock to her boat.

§

Sandy was waiting at the end of the ramp the next morning when I drove up. She let herself into the passenger seat, said "Good morning," and sat back with her eyes closed as I drove her to the courthouse. I knew she was upset over the loss of her marina, but I've always been a person who looks on the bright side, and her negativity was starting to wear on me. In my view, she had escaped death and avoided a possible prison sentence, making her damn lucky the way I saw it. She couldn't look past her losses to see all that she had gained.

The short ride to court didn't take long, and we walked up to the hallway outside the courtroom to meet Walter Lord with the others. He wanted to let us know which of them would go first.

"Bob, you'll be on the stand first to talk about the Bait Shack. Remember to emphasize how long the business has supported you and what your options will be without it." He turned to Carol Cox. "Carol, you'll be next to talk about the diner. I also want to bring up that your last restaurant in South Carolina was taken by eminent domain, and that the property has been a vacant lot for more than fifteen years since then. It makes this action against your diner look even worse."

"You don't have to tell me that. I can't believe this is happening to us again."

He turned to Sandy. "You'll testify last. Talk about coming to this country with the dream of your own business, and how you have everything you own invested in it, including the loan from your parents."

She stared at him with hollow eyes. "Do you think it will do any good?"

"It's a solid strategy. First we show the jury how many people and businesses this action is hurting, then we hit them with Dawn. It's our best shot."

I leaned over to him. "We all have confidence in you, Walter. Go get em." With that we walked into the courtroom as a united front.

§

"Call your first witness, counselor."

"We call Bob Johnson to the stand."

Bob did a great job, and I saw my buddy Ben Carlson from the Bradenton Journal scribbling notes furiously during the testimony. I had a feeling we were going to like the press coverage this time around. Carol was next, and it was a tearjerker. She sounded like the grandmotherly type she is, and she was wonderful at describing the diner as the hub of the waterfront community. When she got to the fact that this was the second time they'd lost a business to eminent domain, there wasn't a dry eye in the house. I hoped that Sandy would do half as well.

She took the stand, was sworn in, and Walter began.

"Miss St. Martin, what brought you to this country?"

"I sailed my boat here from the islands where I was born." Polite laughter came from the gallery.

"I'm sorry, I mean why did you come to America, and

specifically to Dolphin River?"

"I grew up around boats, and it has always been my dream to own a marina, a place for fellow boaters to gather and live on the water."

"Why here?"

"Cost of living is very high on St. Martin, and starting a marina there would have been impossible. I read about the Dolphin River Marina in a yachting magazine, and it sounded perfect."

"What made it perfect?"

"It was in an underdeveloped area, and needed a lot of work. I'm not afraid of hard work, and I thought doing much of it myself would help me to afford it."

"And has that worked out?"

"It has been a struggle, but I was getting by."

"When did you first hear about the River Walk project?"

"I only heard of it when they announced it to the newspaper and the TV stations."

"You were not contacted by the property developer or the city prior to the announcement?"

"No, I was not."

"What was your first reaction to the news of the River Walk development?"

"I thought it was a dream come true."

"Tell my why you thought that, Miss St. Martin."

She looked directly at the jury as she answered. "When I came to Dolphin River, no one wanted to be on the waterfront. My marina, the bait shack and the diner were the only businesses, and our customers were the fisherman. We bought here when it was nothing. When the River Walk was announced, we were so excited. New buildings, new customers, real crowds coming to the place where we waited for them." She paused, then turned to stare at the mayor on the bench behind the city attorney's table. "Then he took it all away."

"He being the Mayor, Blackie Ferguson?"

"Yes. The people who work for him told me I would have to move, and then they offered me $400,000 for my marina."

"That sounds like a lot of money. Is it to you?"

"I paid more than that for the marina, and it was closed at the time. I spent a lot to reopen it, and I owe a good bit more than what they've offered, including $200,000 that my parents loaned me for the down payment. If I accepted the city's offer, I'd be broke and in debt."

"Have you attempted to negotiate a better deal with the city?"

"Yes, and they have refused. They told me I have no choice."

Walter looked towards the jury, and said "They told you wrong. No further questions."

The city attorney declined to ask her anything else, wisely deciding it would only make things worse. Then Walter dropped his bomb.

"Your honor, we call Dawn DeLuca to the stand."

Chapter Thirty-Two

"Objection! We don't have any notice of this witness."

"Your honor, Miss DeLuca is an employee of the city who came to us at the last moment. She has been in fear for her life since the deaths of two co-workers, Andy Mays and Curt Stoneham."

"Counsel, I'll allow it, but make sure it's pertinent to this hearing. This is not a criminal proceeding. It's to set a value for the three properties the city is taking through eminent domain."

"Thank you, your honor."

I could see the mayor about to blow a gasket in the gallery, and I knew he was afraid of what his secretary was about to say.

Dawn was sworn in, and Walter approached and stood across from her. "Miss DeLuca, you are the secretary to the mayor of Dolphin River, Blackie Ferguson, correct?"

"Yes, for two years now."

"And in those two years, have you been aware of private meetings between the mayor and Dick Richmond of Dolphin River Partners?"

"Yes. Right before the River Walk was announced he was in the mayor's office several times a week, always with the door shut."

"When did you first become aware of the River Walk project, Miss DeLuca?"

"Around six months before it was announced publicly."

"Did the mayor tell you about it?"

"No, he was trying to keep it a secret from the staff."

"Then who told you about the project?"

She colored, and said "Curt Stoneham, from the Planning Office."

"And why did Mr. Stoneham share this secret with you?"

Dawn had known Walter needed to ask the question, but she still looked miserable having to say it out loud. "We were having an affair. He told me one night in bed."

"What exactly did he tell you?"

"He said that the project was going to bring a lot of money to Dolphin River, and that he was getting a share of it."

"Did he say how he was to get this share?"

"He told me he tipped off a local real estate developer about it, and that he would share in the profits from buying properties cheap before the River Walk was announced."

"Objection, your honor! Not only is this hearsay, but Mr. Stoneham is deceased and cannot defend himself."

"Mr. Lord, I tend to agree. Try a new line of questioning." The judge looked at the court reporter and said "Strike that from the record. Members of the jury, ignore the last series of questions. Counselor, stick to questions where she has direct knowledge of the actions."

"Thank you, your honor." Walter had anticipated this, but the jury was unlikely to forget what they'd heard.

"Miss DeLuca, you were friends with the late Andy Mays, correct?"

"Yes. We met for coffee sometimes and he talked about how frustrated he was with his work in the Planning Office."

"Objection, hearsay."

"Mr. Lord, remember my warning. I won't tell you again."

"Thank you, your honor." Walter walked to the counsel table and pulled out Andy's drawings. "Miss DeLuca, do you recognize these architectural sketches?"

"Yes, Andy showed them to me."

"Andy Mays?"

"Yes, he said he drew them."

"Your honor, I'd like to enter these drawings into evidence." He approached the bench and showed them to the judge, who had no objection.

"Now, Miss DeLuca, what do these drawings show?"

"They show the marina, bait shack and diner with new facades."

"And did he tell you why he drew these?"

"Objection."

"Overruled. I want to hear the answer. Go ahead, Miss DeLuca."

"Andy said he was trying to get his boss, Curt Stoneham, and the mayor to consider leaving those businesses in the River Walk development."

There was an uproar in the courtroom as city attorney Jim Watson thundered "Objection!"

Judge Greenlaw pounded the gavel until silence fell in the courtroom. "Attorneys approach the bench."

Watson spoke first. "Your honor, this claim of Andy Mays intention is the worst kind of hearsay. The witness is saying what his feelings about the project were."

Walter was quick with his rebuttal. "Your honor, Miss DeLuca is testifying about physical evidence that directly contradicts what Mayor Ferguson testified when he said Andy Mays encouraged him to tear down the buildings to put a park and staircase there. Mr. Watson was allowed to ask the mayor about his knowledge of what Andy Mays said, why may I not do the same with Miss DeLuca about these drawings? They clearly show an intention to keep those buildings."

"You have a point, Mr. Lord. I'll allow it for now. Overruled, Mr. Watson."

Walter returned to the front of the witness stand. "Miss DeLuca, did Andy tell you how his ideas were received by Curt Stoneham and by Mayor Ferguson?"

"Yes, he said Curt told him to drop it if he wanted to keep his job."

"And did Mr. Mays withdraw his proposal?"

"No, he told Curt he did, but I made copies of the drawings and put them on the mayor's desk when he was out."

"What was Mayor Ferguson's response when he saw them?"

"He brought them to my desk and asked why they were there. I told him about Andy's plan to include the buildings, and that Curt Stoneham was trying to keep him from pushing it."

"Did he show any interest in the idea?"

"No. He threw them on my desk and told me that Curt was the head of planning, and that if he opposed the idea there must be a good reason."

"No further questions, your honor."

City attorney Jim Watson looked grim, and declined to cross examine her.

"Your honor, I'd like to re-call Mayor Richard Ferguson."

Blackie slowly returned to the witness chair, where he was reminded he was still under oath.

"Mr. Mayor, you testified earlier that Andy Mays approached you with the idea of the park and the staircase, correct?"

"Yes."

"Now we see graphic evidence that he wanted to put new facades on those buildings and include them in the River Walk development. How are both of those things possible?"

Blackie paused, and mumbled "I don't know, maybe he changed his mind."

"Mr. Mayor, please speak up for the court reporter."

"Maybe he changed his mind."

"And what was your reaction when you saw the drawings? Putting new facades on existing buildings would certainly be more economical for the city than tearing them down to build a park and staircase."

"I don't recall."

"You don't recall what you said, or you don't recall seeing the drawings?" The skeptical look on Walter's face as he asked the question said a lot.

"A lot of things come across my desk. I don't remember those drawings."

Walter shifted gears. "Mayor Ferguson, I'd like to show these receipts for travel expenses to San Antonio, Oklahoma City, Portland, Oregon, and Chicago. Did you take those trips?"

"Yes, we went with the economic development committee to see River Walk style projects in those cities."

"These receipts seem awfully small for that type of travel. Why is that?"

"I always try to watch the city budget."

"Isn't it true, Mr. Mayor, that you flew on Dolphin River Partners private jet?"

"Yes, but the city reimbursed DRP for our travel."

Walter pulled out a receipt and held it up as he read it. "Are you saying that the city reimbursed Dolphin River Partners $450 for you to travel to San Antonio by private jet?"

Blackie looked profoundly unhappy. "No. That was for Curt and me both."

"Mayor Ferguson, isn't it true that Dolphin River Partners showered you with luxury travel, expensive meals and what can only be called 'personal entertainment' on these junkets?"

"The city isn't rich. I thought it made sense to accept financial assistance in the planning phase of the project. It's for the benefit of the whole city."

"It certainly hasn't been beneficial to the three businesses the city is bulldozing to build that staircase, has it, Mr. Mayor?"

Ferguson sat silently.

"No further questions, your honor."

§

Walter rested our case with that, and we sat quietly as Judge Greenlaw gave instructions to the jury before sending them out for deliberations. When court was adjourned the seven of us, Walter, the five business owners and me, walked over to the diner across from the courthouse. It was lunchtime so the place was pretty packed, but Walter had arranged for a private room with a divider so we could talk about the case together.

Bob Johnson said, "Walter, you kicked some ass in there."

"Thanks, but don't get too excited until we have a number from the jury. You never know whether they'll side with the city or with the businesses."

Carol Cox added, "How could they not side with us after you showed that the mayor lied? Andy Mays wasn't behind that stupid idea for a park and staircase, that came straight from Dolphin River Partners."

"I agree that things look hopeful, but remember, this is only about how much the city will have to pay for your property. The city has won the eminent domain action, no matter how unfair that seems."

243

"I do not need to be reminded of that," Sandy said, looking unhappy. "How long will we have before they throw us out?"

I held her hand as Walter answered her. "Probably thirty days, possibly forty five."

"And we will get the money right away?" Carol asked.

"If the city appeals the jury award, they have to deposit the full amount with the court. We might be able to get a moving allowance set for you, but you wouldn't get the rest of the money until the appeal is resolved."

"*Merde!* This just keeps getting worse."

"Listen Sandy," I said. "That hearing couldn't have gone much better than it did. Have faith in Walter."

"Will is right, but don't have faith in me, trust in those jurors to do the right thing."

"I suppose there is no other choice." And she was right about that.

Lunch was subdued after the reality check, with the couples talking mostly with each other except for me and Sandy. She sat in silence as I talked with Walter a little about strategy, including asking for attorney fees.

He said, "If the jury gives us a substantial increase over the city's offer, the judge would likely entertain a motion to add attorney fees to the award. It's kind of a way of punishing the city for being unwilling to negotiate." He glanced at Sandy, leaned towards me and said quietly, "If they stick close to the city's original offer, the judge will figure we wasted our own money in the effort."

"Either way, today is the end, right? You said you couldn't handle any appeals."

Walter looked conflicted. "It's like this, Will. If the jury comes back in a big way for the marina and the others, the attorney fees awarded by the court will be pretty substantial. If that happens, there will be money for appeals. I just didn't want to get your hopes up."

"If there's one thing I learned young it's not to count your chickens too early. We'll wait and see what happens."

Just then Walter's pager went off. He glanced at it, then looked back at me. "The wait is over. The jury is back."

Chapter Thirty-Three

We anxiously made the short walk to the courthouse and took up our spot on the first row behind the attorney's table. When all of the parties had returned, the bailiff said, "All rise," and we stood as Judge Greenlaw took the bench.

He gaveled the court into session, and said, "Bring in the jury."

The moment was eerie for me, and I suspected it felt the same for Sandy as she held my hand in a vise-like grip. Twice we'd had to worry about defending ourselves against a murder charge, and it felt like this case was about much more than money. Fortunately for us, it was all that this jury would decide.

The jury filed in, took their seats, and the judge queried the foreman. "Do you have a verdict?"

"Yes, your honor." The bailiff took the note from him and handed it to the judge. I noticed his eyes widen. He then handed it back to the bailiff, who returned it to the jury foreman.

"Please read the jury's verdict."

"We find that the City of Dolphin River did not offer fair compensation to the owners of the three businesses in question. We hereby award the amounts of $975,000 to Bob's Bait Shack, $1.825 million to the Dolphin River Diner, and $2.6 million dollars to the Dolphin River Marina."

There was a stunned silence in the courtroom. The grip Sandy had on my hand intensified to the bone-crushing level and I had to pry her fingers loose. No one spoke as the judge thanked the jury for their service and dismissed them. The mayor and the city attorney both looked like they'd eaten some bad sushi.

Walter stood and said, "Your honor, I would like to make a motion for attorney fees to be added to the jury's award.

"Put your numbers together, Mr. Lord, and have them to me next week." He paused, thought for a minute, and spoke directly to the mayor. "Before I dismiss this court, I would like to say that I am not that surprised by this verdict. The City of Dolphin River seems to have had way too close a relationship with the developer on the River Walk project. The city grossly abused the power of eminent domain in its dealings with these three businesses. The original offer by the city to the property owners left them no choice but to fight for a fair deal, and the city declined every opportunity to settle for something that was fair to both sides. I would suggest the city think twice before appealing this judgement." He slammed the gavel down. "Court is adjourned."

We rose as a group and began hugging each other and

shaking hands. I turned to Walter. "This is amazing. I can't thank you enough."

Sandy added, "I'm the one who should be thanking him. I have a future now."

It wasn't the time to say it, but I wondered if that future included me. I looked up and saw Ben Carlson from the Journal making his way across the courtroom. "Will, congratulations, what a victory! Still going to write that article for *Florida Waterways*?"

I knew he was kidding, since I'd arranged to write the article on spec so I could use the magazine as a cover for my investigating, but I had other ideas. "You know, I just might write that piece. Something tells me the outcome here will make it a lot more interesting."

He laughed. "You have a point there. Anyway, great job by you and your attorney both. Mind if I ask you a few questions for tomorrow's paper?"

"Let me check with my attorney. Walter, any problem with me giving an interview?"

"Be my guest, I've got to get on a flight back to Atlanta."

I shook his hand. "I won't forget this, Walter."

He grinned and said, "We're even now."

I turned to Sandy. "Mind if I take a few minutes for the interview?"

"You go ahead, Will, I'm going to catch a ride back to the marina with Carol and Ron. She made a cake for us, so stop by the diner on your way back." After kissing me on the cheek, she turned and walked out with the Coxes.

Ben asked, "Are you two serious?"

Sighing, I said, "I am. I'm still not sure about Sandy." I'd find out soon enough.

§

The interview took longer than I expected, since Ben wanted to hear all of the details of how I'd uncovered the city's arrangement with Dolphin River Partners. I left a couple of dead bodies out of the story, but gave him most of the rest of it. I felt drained after retelling the whole thing, and I was feeling the long day by the time I walked into the front door of the diner.

"Hey, Will, we were starting to think you weren't coming." Carol's cake sat on the counter, several slices missing. "Sandy got tired of waiting. She said she'd be on her boat when you were done."

I wasn't hungry, but politely accepted a slice of cake. Carol is a great cook, so it wasn't too big a sacrifice. "Did she seem OK?"

"Sandy? She never seems OK these days. You'd think she'd be turning cartwheels after that jury award, but she still looks like she's lost her best friend. Me and Ron are tickled pink, you know. It's hard to believe that we're getting nearly a million dollars after the city offered us $150,000. Karma's a bitch, ain't it?"

I couldn't argue with that. I said my goodbyes, accepted one last hug and walked outside and down the dock to Sandy's boat. I'm not much of a mind reader, but I couldn't help but feel that I wasn't going to like what Sandy had to say. I reached her boat near the end of the dock, and tapped lightly on the side of the cabin. "Sandy?"

"Will, is that you? Come aboard."

I found her sitting in the cabin wrapped in a terry robe with a glass of wine in her hand. "Are you OK?"

"*Oui*. It's just been an emotional day for me."

"It has been for all of us, but now it's over."

"It is not over for me, *mon cheri'*. In a month I will have no business and no home."

I smiled at her. "Seems like having 2.6 million dollars in the bank could ease the sting a little."

"Don't think I am not grateful to you and Walter. You saved my life, and the two of you together rescued me from poverty. I will pay you back for the money you loaned to my marina as soon as I receive the settlement."

"Don't worry about that, Sandy. I haven't."

She smiled and said, "I know you don't care about the money, but I will sleep better knowing you have been repaid."

I took her hand. "I've got a great idea. Why don't we move your boat to SailFin Point near me, and you and I can take a long vacation. We both need it, and now we can afford to."

"I cannot leave the people here. Eduardo will need my help in closing things down, and the dock tenants will begin leaving as they find places to go. It would be unfair to desert them."

'We can wait until the marina is closed then." She put her glass down as I pulled her into an embrace. "I want us to have time alone together, to heal from the stress of the last few months. To work on 'us'." She was stiff in my arms, and I leaned back and held her at arms length. "Sandy, why do I feel that you don't like this idea?"

"I didn't want to tell you today. Not after all you've done for me."

I braced myself. "Tell me what?"

"After the marina is closed, I am going back to St. Martin."

Exasperated, I said, "You know I can't just pick up and move to St. Martin, I have a life here, and so do you."

"My life was the marina and my boat."

Ouch, that hurt.

"Now the marina will be gone, and this boat is ruined for me. I will never be aboard it again without thinking of death and loss."

"You didn't include me in there anywhere, I noticed."

"I'm so sorry, Will, I did not mean to hurt you. Our time together has been wonderful, but now it's time for me to go."

There wasn't a lot to say to that. I stood and moved towards the door, and she rushed in front of me. "Do not hate me, please. I couldn't stand for you to hate me." Tears ran down her face, and I leaned in and kissed her softly.

"I could never hate you, Sandy. A part of me will always love you." I pulled away from her, opened the cabin door and stepped onto the deck of the boat.

The walk down the dock seemed a mile long, and when I got in my car I put the top down and drove slowly back to my boat. I felt like burning rubber out of the parking lot, but hell, the gravel would do a number on my paint. If I kept telling myself she wasn't worth it, maybe I'd start believing it.

What started out as an evening of celebration was shaping up to be a long and lonely night.

Chapter Thirty-Four

My lonely night turned into a week, and then into three more. Living in a boat on the water is like having the world as your front porch, but when all you do is sleep late and start drinking early, that world gets a lot smaller. It didn't take long for green spots to grow on the unwashed decks in the same way that the dark shadows grew under my eyes.

It was ironic, really. I'd become a local hero for saving Sandy, Bob and Carol from getting completely screwed by the city, and the latter two and their spouses couldn't thank me enough. Bob kept my freezer stocked with filets of redfish he'd caught. Now that he was retired, there was more time for fishing. Carol brought me food from her kitchen every couple of days because she knew I wasn't going out, and I'd managed to put on a few pounds in spite of my hermit act. Only problem was, the one person I'd done it all for was gone.

Sandy had packed up and sailed off in her boat without even coming to say goodbye. I'd gotten a text from her, saying she was leaving and that she would always love me, but that seeing me again was too painful. I had become a reminder of Andy Mays and Mardy Jackson, of losing her marina. You might think that the 2.6 million dollars I'd helped her get from the city would soften the loss, but apparently it didn't.

After the onslaught of bad publicity that fell on the city from the jury's verdict, the city attorney had strongly advised the mayor and city council not to appeal the judgement. Dolphin River had been forced to take out a loan against future tax revenues, and they had paid the money. The cost came to more than six million dollars after the judge had added in attorney fees. Walter had profited nicely from his generous offer to take on the case pro bono as a favor to me, and I was happy for him.

Hell, I was happy for everybody but myself. It took a visit from Captain Rick to snap me out of my funk.

"Hey there, Will, permission to come aboard?" I was sitting on the rear deck in a dirty tee shirt and shorts, finishing my first cup of coffee, even though it was nearly noon.

"Sure, Rick. Want some coffee?"

"No thanks, I had my two cups a few hours ago." He looked at me for a minute, and said "You're looking a little rough there, Will." He was actually being kind. I looked like crap, and I knew it.

"I haven't had much energy lately, that's all."

He looked skeptical at my lame excuse. "Oh, come on, everybody on this dock knows you're pining away over Sandy. I know what it means to lose someone you love, but you've mourned long enough. She's not dead, she chose to leave."

"That's part of why it hurts so much."

"Look, as long as you sit here wallowing in your sadness, it's not going to get any better. Get out, go for a walk, get your blood moving again." He wrinkled his nose, and said "And you might start by taking a shower."

This was embarrassing. "OK, Rick, I promise. No more licking my wounds, OK?"

He grinned at me. "Get a shower, clean up this grungy boat, and you might find a girl to help you with that. You'd be surprised at how the ladies around here have been talking about you since you pulled off that miracle against the city. Now that they know you're unattached, I've heard more than a few who said they were interested. Of course, they haven't seen you like this."

"OK, OK, I got it. Shower, cleanup and exercise. I'm not ready to meet women though."

"Every man feels that way occasionally, at least until they meet one."

"I'll take that under advisement, OK, Rick?"

He stood up, tipped his cap and left without another word. I looked at the cold coffee in my cup, went in to the galley and dumped it in the sink. The counter was covered with dirty dishes and the wrappings from the food Carol had delivered. It was going to take a while to wash it all, but I decided to use the hot water for a shower first. I grabbed a bottle of icy water from the fridge, gulped it down and made my way to the head in my cabin.

Brushing my teeth first, I flossed while the water heated up, then stripped and got in the shower. It's unusually spacious for a boat, and I thought briefly about how nice it would be to have a woman in there me with me to scrub my back.

Maybe there was still life in me after all. I took a long shower and ran out the hot water, dried my hair and prepared to shave off the beard that had managed to cover my chin in the last month. Then I reconsidered. You don't see many beards in Florida because of the heat, but I thought it suited me. Instead of shaving I trimmed it neatly, then put on a fresh pair of shorts and a tee shirt and switched my flip-flops for some closed front sandals. I went to the main cabin, threw back all the curtains and flooded the space with light. The pile of dishes was an embarrassment, but they'd have to wait for more hot water. Instead, I'd take another piece of Rick's advice and go for a walk.

The bright sun outside drove me back in to fetch my sunglasses, which was probably a good idea anyway as they hid my puffy eyes. I started the walk with my own dock, where I was greeted like a long-lost friend by quite a few of my neighbors. Patty, who lived with her two Yorkies on an old Chris-Craft houseboat, was the first.

"Will! I haven't seen you in ages. I'd have thought you moved if it wasn't for your boat still being docked here."

"Yeah, I haven't been getting out much lately."

She gave me a wry grin. "That's an understatement. I got used to seeing you out working on your boat and washing that cute little car, and I know it's been more than a month since you did either one."

Geez, I guess this was my day to get embarrassed by everyone I ran into. "Guess I'll have to get caught up on my chores; don't want to make the neighborhood look bad."

She reached out and touched my arm. "Hey, I'm just teasing you a little. I heard you'd been having a bad time; I'm glad to see you getting out again."

"Thanks Patty, it's good to know people care." I continued my walk, making my way to other docks where I was less likely to be recognized. Explaining the reason for my withdrawal wasn't something I felt comfortable doing, and it was easier to walk in silence. Since SailFin Point has more than a dozen docks, I got plenty of time to stretch my legs and feel the sun on my back.

By the time I made my way back to the WanderLust, I had to admit that I felt better. That feeling evaporated when I walked into the salon and was confronted with the piles of dishes in the galley. It was starting to smell, something that I had failed to notice earlier. Guess since I'd been ignoring my own odor, the dishes weren't going to bother me. Now, after an hour's walk in the fresh air, the sour smell in the boat seemed oppressive. I threw open the windows and began the slow process of washing up in the smallish sink. Even though the WanderLust is luxuriously spacious compared to most liveaboard boats at the marina, it was still a boat, and that made for smaller sinks and counters than your average apartment kitchen.

After an hour the worst of it was done, and my back was sore from bending over the sink. I dried and stacked the clean dishes, took out the trash, and decided to reward myself with dinner at the RiverHouse restaurant on the water. I cleaned myself up, swapped my tee for a flowered shirt and made the short walk to the restaurant. The night was mild, and I asked for a table outside by the channel facing the breakwater. Watching the boats come and go in the twilight was restful, and that was exactly what I was looking for tonight.

After ordering the lobster pot pie I sipped a bourbon while tourists tossed bread to seagulls nearby, starting a battle for the stray crumbs. The gulls threatened to disturb the entire waterfront before they finally tired of the game and flew away. As the silence returned, I heard a voice behind me.

"I see you decided to take my advice."

"Hey, Rick. Yes I did, have a seat."

"Feel better too, don't ya?" He was grinning as he said it.

"You were right, as usual. I confess, I didn't realize quite how bad I'd let things get. It's going to take me at least a week to get the boat and my car looking decent again."

"Good for you, Will. By the time you're finished, things will look a lot brighter, I'd wager."

"No more arm twisting, I'm doing it. Maybe I'll even take the WanderLust out for a cruise when I'm done. I met Sandy shortly after I moved aboard last year, and I haven't really gone anywhere since."

"Glad to hear it. Let me know if you need somebody to help you steer that big tub."

"You've got a deal, Rick."

§

It took a lot longer than a week to get everything in order with my boat, closer to a month. You wouldn't think things could go to pot that quickly, but between the salt water, the Florida sun and the humidity, the WanderLust had suffered. I could have afforded to hire others to do the work, but doing it myself was a form of penance for neglecting her. I took the easy way out with my Z4, letting the BMW dealer pick it up for a scheduled service and a wash, wax and detailing. While it was gone I made a deal with the marina to let me put an aluminum roof over my usual parking space to keep it out of the sun. Gary, the manager, had at first refused, but when I had offered to build one big enough for him to keep his classic Porsche 911 next to my Beemer he came around. Funny how that works.

Captain Rick had stayed after me ever since I'd thrown out the possibility of taking a cruise on the WanderLust, and it was finally time. I stocked the boat with provisions and good beer, and Rick brought the latest charts for the waters we'd be cruising. The route would take us down the IntraCoastal along the West Coast, past Longboat Key and Siesta Key. Next we'd move into the deeper waters of the Gulf to avoid the manatee zones from Venice Inlet down to Pine Island Sound. We'd then stay in open water past Cape Romano and Cape Sable to Key West. After a few days in the craziness that is sometimes called 'Key Weird', we'd putter around the rest of the keys before heading back towards Bradenton and home.

Not exactly a cruise across the Atlantic, but hey, you've got to start somewhere. As we disconnected the water and power from the dock, cranked the twin diesels and cast off the lines, the flutter in my chest was one of excitement. I hadn't realized how stale I'd become living at the dock in a boat that was meant for travel. Rick stood next to me on the flybridge as we slowly maneuvered past the rows of sailboats, halyards ringing as they tapped the aluminum masts in the breeze, and it sounded like applause. It was great to be back at the helm, blue skies and calm seas ahead. I said a silent prayer of thanks, and hit the throttles as we moved into the channel.

Epilogue

The trip we'd planned on lasting a week lasted for three, and we returned to SailFin Point and slip F-11 tanned, rested and full of enthusiasm. The trip had deepened my friendship with Captain Rick, and he'd forgiven me for keeping the secret about Andy Mays, but with one caveat.

"Will, from now on, anything that you get into with your investigating, we're partners, OK?"

"I don't plan on *doing* any more investigating, unless it's to write a story. The whole thing with the eminent domain case only came up because I was trying to help a friend, and I learned my lesson on that."

"You know Sandy leaving wasn't just about the bad memories, don't you?"

I wasn't sure what he meant. "It wasn't?"

"As soon as she got here I knew she wouldn't stay forever. Have you forgotten the name of her boat? *Au Revoir* should have told you where her heart was."

"Well, whatever her reason was, I'm swearing off relationships." His raised eyebrow told me he was skeptical. "I mean it, Rick. I'm not saying I won't find female companionship, but I'll make it clear we're just having fun. No entanglements."

"Famous last words."

"Which ones, no more investigating or no more entanglements?"

Rick was grinning. "Both."

§

The following week I had settled back into dock life, doing my little boat maintenance projects in the morning, then going for a walk and a swim before a leisurely lunch. I should have known it was too good to last.

I was just finishing my lunch of roast beef on crusty bread with swiss cheese, a healthy dollop of spicy mustard topping it off, and was washing it down with an icy Red Stripe when I heard Captain Rick on the dock.

"Hey, Will, you on board?"

"Sure, Rick, come on in."

"You decent? I'm not alone."

Now I was curious. "Decent enough." I was still in my swimsuit, but grabbed a tee shirt and slipped it over my head just before the cabin door opened. Backlit by the sun, I could see long hair atop the silhouette of a very curvy body. Rick stepped in behind her.

"Will Harper, meet Molly Warner, she's Mack Wilson's granddaughter. He lives on dock nine in that old sailboat."

"Yes, I remember talking to him at the fish fry. Nice to

meet you, Molly." I ushered them into the salon and they took a seat on the settee across from my chair. She looked very unhappy and nervous, and sat silently.

"Molly, if Will's going to help you, you've got to talk to him."

Uh oh, I thought.

She put her hands together in her lap and began speaking. "It's my husband, Daniel, he's been arrested."

"What for?"

Now she looked really miserable. "We only had the one car, and I was in a wreck that was my fault. Danny had no way to get to work at the boatyard, so he borrowed some money from a guy at work to buy an old motorcycle he found on Craig's List. The people he bought it from said there was no tag on it because their kid had been riding it in their yard, but they gave him one that was expired. Danny put it on there anyway. He figured it wouldn't stand out as much as having no tag at all, and he had to wait for payday to go get a new tag."

She was trying not to cry, and I gave her a tissue. "Why did he get arrested?"

"The first day he rode it to work, he got pulled over for the expired tag, and they said it was stolen."

"The motorcycle was stolen?"

"No, just the tag."

OK, now I was curious. "And they arrested him for that?"

"Yes sir, theft of a motor vehicle ID. It's a felony charge."

"Seems like a decent lawyer could get him off on that. Have you talked to an attorney?"

Rick chimed in. "Mack's trying to get money together to get the boy a lawyer, but that's not the only problem. Molly, tell him the rest."

"When they arrested him he had to sign a release that they could search our trailer. The cops came and pretty much tore things up, and didn't find anything. Then they searched the shed out back, and when they were done they took a big bag full of stuff out of there. I asked what they were taking, but they wouldn't tell me. Now they're saying there was meth in there." She wiped a tear from her cheek, and said, "Mr. Harper, Danny and I never did drugs, and we sure wouldn't sell them. I mean, we smoked some pot before, but no *real* drugs."

"Will, Mack told me Danny's been saving money to finish college and go to law school. Unless we can figure out who's behind this, his life will be ruined."

I did *not* need this. "Molly, I'm sorry, but I'm not a private investigator, I'm a writer. It sounds to me like you need a good lawyer, someone with a staff to do the investigating."

She was crying again, and Rick patted her on the shoulder. "Molly, the boat's bathroom is right through there, why don't you go wash your face and let me talk to Will for a minute." She stumbled toward the head, shut the door and left us in silence.

I was fuming. Rick knew I'd said no more of this, and here he was with a teary female pleading for my help.

"Listen, Rick..."

He cut me off quickly. "No, you listen. After what happened to you and Sandy, you owe Karma a little payback. She came out of that rich and you came out of it with your freedom. It could have easily gone the other way, and there'd be an empty slip where we're sitting. There's something rotten going on here, and I don't know anybody better than you at digging up who's behind it. We've got to help this girl."

I could read between the lines. Karma wasn't the only one needing payback. I owed Rick for what I'd put him through, the burden I left him carrying. Well, shit.

"OK Rick, I'm in."

Postscript

One of my reasons for writing this book is that some readers may be unaware of the prevalence in the United States of municipalities using the power of eminent domain to confiscate the property of citizens for the benefit of private developers.

The book you've just read is a murder mystery, a work of complete fiction. All of the characters and the situations they find themselves in are fictional. No connection to any real person is intended or implied.

§

This is what really did happen in Greenville, South Carolina.

In the fall of 2003, the City of Greenville decided to remove three buildings on South Main Street housing a stereo store, the home and office of an architect, and another business.

266

The land would be used to build a staircase to access the River Falls Park, which was being redeveloped by the city.

In early 2004, Hughes Development announced a $65 million dollar development featuring restaurants, a hotel, a four-story fountain, a parking garage and space for local artists along the river front. The drawings of the project showed the view of the beautiful new buildings with the older buildings of the three owners on South Main having vanished.

The three building's owners, particularly stereo store owner Billy Mitchell, fought back hard against what they saw as an effort by the city to give their property to private developers. The offers the city made to purchase the property were rejected by the owners, and the case went to court.

In January 2005 the power of eminent domain won, and the owners watched as the three buildings were demolished. They had not yet been paid for the property.

In early 2006, a jury awarded more than $1.8 million dollars to Billy Mitchell, and nearly a million dollars to the Surratt family. A second jury awarded $2.6 million dollars to architect Verne Cassaday for the loss of his home and office. The amounts awarded were considerably higher than the offers the City of Greenville had previously made for the properties.

The city declined to appeal, and the owners were paid.

Links to the documents verifying this information are posted at my web site, www.crosbystills.com, under the heading Million Dollar Staircase.

A Favor, Please...

Thanks for reading my book, Million Dollar Staircase. I hope you enjoyed reading it as much as I enjoyed writing it. Please take a moment to leave a short review on the book's Amazon page at http://tiny.cc/8p1m7x. If you have any trouble finding it there, a link is on the main menu bar at my website, www.crosbystills.com. The review only needs to be a few words, or heck, even one word if you're short of time. It helps me to reach other readers and to be able to keep writing, so Thank You in advance!

I'm currently hard at work on the next title in the Will Harper Mystery series, tentatively titled Guilty Money, and if you'd be interested in receiving an advance copy when it's completed, e-mail me at david@crosbystills.com. Also feel free to write me if you have comments or questions about the book, or if there are any errors I have missed that you'd like to point out. Authors and editors can't catch everything, so your help is appreciated.

Happy Reading,

David Crosby
Writing from the wilds of Leesburg, Florida

Made in the USA
Las Vegas, NV
21 March 2023

69453033R00163